A VERY PRIVATE ISLAND

BY J.D. KRUEGER

© J.D. KRUEGER 2021

1

Massive hands closed around the girl's neck. Cold palms like sandpaper. She twisted away, but there was nowhere to go. The boat was small and going fast—the water black and smooth like a polished piece of coal. The night made land impossible to see; houses lit the bay like distant stars.

Her hair whipped in the wind; fear paralyzed her. The roar of the engine muffled her screams. She curled in the corner of the boat as the man walked toward her. Like a giant, his wide stance kept him balanced as the speed boat bounced up and down across the sea.

Regret engulfed her now. All the choices she shouldn't have made that lead her to this very moment. She wanted a warm bed and to see her friends again. She prayed to god. She had never prayed before.

She grabbed the silver dove pendant around her neck. For a moment, it comforted her, gave her hope. She was going to live. She had to. If she jumped into the water, she would survive; she knew that. The water wasn't that cold, and she was a good swimmer. The night was clear, the sea was calm. She could follow the lights and make it to shore.

Sharks? What about the sharks? But what about the monster marching toward her now?

She winced and squeezed the pendant. She was going to jump. The girl stood up and readied herself. She frantically put her hand down for balance. Her ring caught the necklace and snapped it.

She watched as the silver dove pendant bounced off the back of the boat and disappeared into the darkness.

Dark, murky waters sped by. She was all alone.

Deadened with fear, she attempted to steady herself—the reverberation of the boat vibrating beneath her feet. The man stood in front of her. Behind him, the island glowed in the darkness. She wanted to cry. Jumping was her only option now. She prayed she could make it to shore. Black water splashed against the boat. The moonlight jagged and rough flickered across the water.

She glanced for a life vest—nothing. The man lunged.

She leaped from the boat.

Her head smashed the side of the boat before she tumbled into the sea. The water felt like concrete as she skidded across. She attempted to steady herself in the water, but the waves were too strong and it was colder than she thought.

The girl glanced for the boat, for shore, for anything. A wave crashed over her and salt filled her mouth. She didn't want to go, she didn't want to leave. Then another crash of water and salt. She was cold except for the warm blood oozing from the cut in her head. She tried to swim but felt weak.

Another wave crashed on her. She took a deep breath but got cold saltwater. She started to shake, the distant roar of the boat engine faded away and everything went black.

2

The crystal clear blue water sparkled like confetti. It was dawn in the Pillsbury Sound, the four-mile stretch of Caribbean sea that lies between the US Virgin Islands of St. Thomas and St. John.

Boats carrying tourists from the cruise ships or island resorts jetted out from the more populated St. Thomas on fishing or dive excursions. The opposite island was St. John, which remained calm and quiet.

Among the lush green shores, mega-mansions were scattered, while the rest of St. John was designated a national park--donated by the Rockefellers in 1956.

In addition to the two larger Virgin Islands, the Pillsbury Sound was made up of numerous smaller islands, some private and some uninhabited. They scattered the water and disappeared into the horizon, fading into the most tranquil and perfect sea blue.

Anchored in the water off the coast of St. Thomas was an old skiff. The boat slowly bobbed up and down. The waves caressed its flaking blue hull, which read: JONI'S DIVE SHOP in a rust-colored red.

Cubby holes where diving tanks, masks, and snorkels should have been were vacant. The extended plank seating where divers put on their equipment took on the occasional splash of seawater and sea breeze.

Empty Bud Light cans scattered across the deck were crunched down to small saucers to stop them from rolling around, forming a trail leading to a human foot sticking out of the cabin.

The radio next to the steering wheel crackled. "Jimmy," a nervous voice said.

A moan came from the cabin, and a toe twitched.

"People are here," the panicked voice cracked from the radio again. "Pick up. Where the hell are you?"

A voice groaned from the cabin and the foot began to flail. Beer cans scattered across the deck.

Jimmy Walsh sat up and wiped his eyes. He placed his sunglasses dangling from the strap around his neck over his tan face, fitting just like a puzzle piece.

Jimmy grabbed the radio and mumbled the words into one long sentence, "Just having a little engine trouble. Be there in a sec."

"Jesus, Jimmy," came the response through the radio. "Just get here."

Jimmy returned the radio to its hanger and laid back down. He knew Joni would give him shit, he just couldn't handle it now. His head throbbed. His throat was dry and crinkled like an autumn leaf. He was too hungover to go anywhere or talk to anyone, let alone get into an argument with the big boss.

He tapped the breast pocket of his Hawaiian shirt and pulled out his cigarettes. Lying on his back, he lit one, inhaled, and then slowly got up. Even with his sunglasses on, he still needed to squint at the bright tropical sun. He found his flip flops amongst the confetti of Bud Light cans and slipped them on.

Jimmy spent the next five minutes wondering if he would fall over or vomit. When his sea legs returned, he picked up the beer cans and hauled in the anchor. Jimmy turned the ignition and a large plume of black smoke coughed out the back. He headed back toward St. Thomas.

The morning salty air was the best way to cure a hangover, plus a few Tylenol washed down with a leftover beer. At forty-two, Jimmy Walsh seemed to wake up more often than not in a relatively similar shape. Most of the time, it was back at the dive shop on a beach chair or the dock, but he always preferred the boat—no guilt in the morning and the fresh Caribbean breeze to coax him back to life. Jimmy knew he was going to catch hell when he got back. He could hear the screech of Joni's voice in his head already, but she would never fire him. She annoyed more people down at the marina than he did, plus she couldn't dive to save her ass.

3

Joni Haven was freakin' out. She had all the dive equipment already on the dock and was trying to make up whatever excuse she could to the five college bros on why their deadbeat dive instructor was late.

Joni offered them juice and chips, and promised that Jimmy Walsh would show them a great time. She talked Jimmy up, saying, "He was the best diver on the island, and a great captain." She wasn't lying—he was, she was just leaving out the part that he was an asshole who never listened.

Joni's Dive Shop was buried in the thick ferns way past the fancy resort area. Surrounded by palm trees, the dive shop was secluded and located down a long dirt road that even many island locals didn't know existed.

A rusted barbed wire fence surrounded the property that consisted of one small poorly-constructed cement building, and a seemingly endless amount of "island-junk," as Jimmy referred to it. Rotting boats and old cars Joni'd hoarded over the years were scattered everywhere. Joni, a massive woman nearing seventy didn't really care anymore. That's why she paid Jimmy. The one saving grace of the property was its dock and beautiful view of the Pillsbury Sound. St. John was directly across the water.

"He had to pick up a few things," Joni said to the college bros, who were now lying on the dock sunning themselves.

Jimmy tossed Joni a line as he pulled the dive boat into the dock.

"Where have you been?" Joni asked, making sure to keep her voice down so the clients wouldn't hear. "They must have been waiting forty minutes."

Jimmy scratched his head. "This damn engine—"

"You smell like a bar," Joni shot back and quickly began to pass Jimmy the dive equipment.

"I'm sure the frat boys won't care."

Joni rolled her eyes. "You need a piece of gum."

"But I haven't finished my cigarette yet."

"I don't care." Joni pulled the cigarette from Jimmy's lips and tossed it in the water. She handed him a piece of gum.

"That's littering." Jimmy watched his cigarette sink into the water.

Joni gave Jimmy her shut-the-fuck-up stare.

"I know that look." Jimmy chewed on the gum and scanned the grounds. "Some could make the argument that you can't actually litter at the dump."

"Ha-ha, very funny. You know you get paid to clean this up."

"No, I get paid to manage it." Jimmy began pointing at different portions of the property. "That's trash pile A, that's pile B." Jimmy paused. "What's up with that?" A man stood on a step ladder installing a security camera at the front of the property.

Joni finished passing Jimmy the remainder of the equipment and said, "Damn kids stealing my gas. I'm gonna catch them."

"Gas—the only thing of value here."

"What about that?" Joni pointed to an old sailboat amongst the ferns. "It's a god damn antique."

"You sure about that?"

Joni had had enough of Jimmy. "You're lucky I let you sleep on my boat."

"Yea, yea, and you're lucky I do all the work so you can sleep all day."

"You don't know how good you have it, Jimmy."

"Likewise."

"Always an asshole."

Jimmy winked, "Love you too, honey."

"All right, guys," Joni said to the college guys sunning themselves on the dock. "Let's go diving,"

She glanced at Jimmy. "I'll be in my office."

"Sleeping?" Jimmy grinned.

"Damn right," Joni said and walked toward the small cement structure in the middle of the property.

Jimmy quickly strapped in the remainder of the equipment and turned on his charm for the tourists.

"Sorry about that guys, damn engine trouble."

"You sure everything is okay?" One of the college guys said, moving his sunglasses down. He appeared nervous about getting on the boat "We don't want to get out there and have to paddle back."

Jimmy pulled the young guy on the boat. "Are you kidding? I fixed it. This thing is a beauty, it runs like a charm. All you have to worry about is having a great time. Couldn't have asked for a better day. No clouds, no waves, the visibility is damn near perfect."

Jimmy started up the boat. The engine gurgled to life and they pulled away from the dock.

Twenty minutes later the dive boat sped through the brilliant blue water as they traveled to the dive site. Jimmy relished the Caribbean and his job. The charm, the ocean. It all felt like a clean slate. It didn't matter what occurred the day, the week or even years before. Every day was a fresh start. The ocean had no memory or judgement.

"Fuckin' awesome, man," one of the frat boys yelled at the top of his lungs before chest bumping his buddy. "That's it, I'm movin' here for good."

Jimmy couldn't blame them. "First time in the Caribbean?"

"Yes, we're staying in Red Hook," the guy said. Red Hook was the tourist hub on this side of the island. Quiet and quant but still a great place to party. "Two more days and then it's back to my cubicle and twenty degree weather."

"I don't miss that." Jimmy never forgot the winters he left behind.

"You from here?" the guy asked.

"New England."

"Big move."

Jimmy shrugged, then laughed. "I guess. I hate the snow...well, unless it's in a blender with some rum."

"You been here for a while?"

"Ten years," Jimmy yelled over the sound of the engine, "and I haven't regretted it one day."

Suddenly a helicopter buzzed by the top of the boat. The college kid fell backward, startled by how close it came to the boat.

"Jesus," the kid yelled, getting to his feet. "Who's that, the President?"

"Maybe." Jimmy took a hand off the steering wheel and pointed straight ahead. A small, lush green, privately owned island emerged from the blue water. "Little Saint George. They're always having conferences or parties there. It's a private island, so no reporters. All the big shots just fly in and fly out."

"What for?"

"No clue. Save the world type of shit."

"You really think it could be the President?"

"Why not? He's been here before, and so have the other ones."

"Who owns it?"

"Someone with more money than god." Jimmy let up on the throttle of the boat and it began to slow down. "We're almost there. Start getting ready."

Jimmy drove the small dive boat into the island cove of Little St. George and dropped anchor.

Once all the divers had all their gear Jimmy strolled down the center of the boat checking to make sure their dive equipment was secured correctly and working. Joni had always nagged him about the liability of being a dive boat captain. Scuba diving was one of the few things Jimmy took seriously and was annoyed when Joni tried to make like he didn't know better.

"Weight good?" Jimmy asked one of the divers tugging on his weight belt.

"Hope so. I think I've put on a few pounds since last time I dove."

Jimmy always double-checked their gear and asked questions twice. He wanted everyone to feel safe. Most of the time tourists only dove when they were on vacation, so a year gap was not uncommon.

"Looks good to me." Jimmy slapped one of the guys on the back. "The last thing we need is for any of you to get the bends. Ruin your vacation having to spend a week in a decompression chamber the size of a coffin."

"Is that what really happens?" one of the tourists chirped. He didn't seem nervous, just curious.

"Sure is. All your buddies will be crushin' margaritas on the beach while you're sipping water though a straw. No fun."

"You dive this spot often?"

"Could do it with my eyes closed."

"Good enough for me," one of the guys said before jumping into the water.

The rest of the divers waddled liked penguins from the weight of their tanks to the back of the boat, put on their fins and dove in. Jimmy followed.

Jimmy made the "okay" sign once they were all in the water with their BCDs inflated and breathing through their regulators. Every diver replied with the same hand gesture. Jimmy then gave a thumbs down —the dive signal to go underwater and one by one the divers descended.

Just as Jimmy was about to deflate his BCD and descend a man on the shore of Little St. George caught his eye. Jimmy though it was strange. He wore khaki pants and seemed to be staring right at him through binoculars.

The thought of the man with the binoculars quickly left his mind like everything else on the surface once Jimmy was underwater. The divers followed the boat anchor to the bottom of the ocean—eighty feet down.

Visibility was near pristine. White rolling sand covered the bottom of the sea like a soft blanket. Tiny fish bounced around in a frenzy, fearing the barracuda that hovered above them. The circle of life was in full effect.

Jimmy accounted for all the divers and pointed in the direction they were going to swim. Jimmy glanced at his Shearwater dive computer on his wrist. The small dive watch strapped to his arm allowed him to keep track of the whole dive: depth, time, air and most importantly navigation.

Jimmy led the team past unique types of aquatic life. Jimmy was swift to point out the various kinds of fish and coral. He didn't know if the other divers cared —they probably didn't, but it was the fun part of his job.

Ten minutes later an old World War II shipwreck emerged from the cyan water. The massive grey hull rested at the depths of the sea like a gravesite. Jimmy fell back and hung at the sea bed while the other divers moved by him to examine the wreck.

The vessel teemed with life. After all these years eroding at the bottom of the ocean it had become an artificial reef. Crabs scurried along the frame, while eels slithered in and out of portholes.

A shimmer from the white sand below caught Jimmy's eye. He drifted a little closer, guessing it was some fish he didn't recognize. Jimmy adjusted his swimming pattern as he grew near, careful not to kick up sand and cloud his view or frighten away whatever was buried.

Soon he realized it wasn't a fish, but jewelry.

He had discovered items from the surface on dives before, but nothing of any value. Jimmy reached down and scooped up the piece of jewelry. It was a necklace, silver perhaps, stunning and seemingly expensive. It wasn't old, and couldn't have been on the bottom of the sea long. Jimmy moved it closer for a better look so it was in front of his mask. On the end of the necklace was a small silver pendant in the shape of a dove.

Jimmy twisted the pendant in his finishers. There was something haunting about it.

Why was it here?

What happened?

It seemed far too important to have just been lost, discarded. There had to be a story, however, Jimmy knew, like many relics discovered in the ocean, they could remain a mystery forever.

4

"Great dive, man." The college bro with the big head said as he took off his gear and poured himself a rum punch from the plastic cooler on the deck of the boat.

A cigarette dangled from Jimmy's lips as he secured all the diving gear. "That's one of my favorite spots. A lot of fish down there today." He had dove the site multiple times but have never anchored this close to the island. Jimmy rubbed the dove pendant in his pocket and glanced at the shore of Little Saint George. The man with the binoculars and khaki pants was gone, or at least gone from site.

"You see something?"

Jimmy shook his head and started the engine. "No, just admiring the view."

"Can we get on that island and hang with the rich?" one of the guys joked.

"I wish, unfortunately we're not invited. But something tells me that won't stop you guys from having a good time." Jimmy snagged a bottle of Captain Morgan's from the cooler and topped each of their rum punches off. "Cherry on top."

The divers cheered. "Speaking of a good time Jimmy, can you hook us up? You know what I mean?"

Jimmy laughed and lit another cigarette and piloted the boat back toward St. Thomas. "No, what do you mean?" He knew exactly what they meant. After all, drugs were the third most popular pastime in the Caribbean after drinking and sex. Drinking was always first. He got a kick out of watching the kid squirm as he thought how to ask the question.

"Well...we ahh..." one of the other kids chimed in. "We want to continue having a good time. We only have two days left...and we ahh were wondering...if..."

Jimmy grinned. He had let them fidget enough. He knew his hard-living face had drug dealer written all over it. "Ahh...I...see. Pot?" he said without taking his eyes off the path back to the dive shop.

"Not really..." the guy shouted over the engine.

"Coke? Ecstasy? Molly?" Jimmy stopped playing games and began listing off drugs like a pharmacist. Cocaine seemed to be their drug of choice.

"You have any?" the kid with the big head asked. His tense shoulders relaxing at the thought of having his vacation end with a bang.

"No, I stay away from the stuff." Jimmy tossed his cigarette into the water as he pulled into the dive shop dock.

The kid tensed up. "Sorry, man. Yeah, me too. It's just my friends. I didn't even mean to ask you. I was just curious."

"I just meant me." Jimmy calmed them down as he tied the boat to the dock. "I know a guy who can help you."

"Really?"

"Really," Jimmy said. He was actually "the guy," but he had a system down. Pretend to act as a middle man and never get his name involved with any of that stuff.

The local law enforcement never seemed to pry or get wind of his little side hustle, but he knew cops, especially island cops. If you make too much of a scene, all of a sudden where the police once turned a blind eye, would instead turn a spotlight.

"How much you looking for?" Jimmy asked. His method was simple: walk into the dive shop cement building, grab the customers drug of choice and put it by the fence under the rock and say the "local drug dealer has dropped off their package," and then tell them "please replace the package with the money."

It wasn't a foolproof operation. Any idiot if they thought hard enough could guess Jimmy was their guy, but most people didn't. They were on vacation and were just happy to get their drugs.

After tying the boat off Jimmy strolled into the building. Joni was sound asleep. Her feet up on her desk with headphones so big they looked like earmuffs. Jimmy tiptoed past her into the back locker room where they kept all their supplies: oxygen tanks, BCDs, flippers, and masks. Jimmy promptly opened the combination lock for his locker and reached inside. He unzipped a leather shaving bag. Inside were small plastic baggies evenly distributed with pills, powder, and pot.

He stuffed two of the powered bags in his pocket and quietly went to the door.

"Jimmy," Joni said. Her eyes still closed like she was sleeping. "Whatever you're doing on the side, I don't want to know. You hear me? I don't want to know," she said, emphasizing each syllable.

"You're in luck, because I'm not doing anything."

"That's what I thought."

"Just out of curiosity, is that security camera up and running yet?"

"Tomorrow."

"Good to know."

There was a specific unspoken rule about all transplants to the Caribbean: silence. Everyone had secrets and Jimmy was no different. There was never prying or gossiping about the past. Jimmy knew Joni was from somewhere down south and she had been married once, and she knew he had been from Boston and had once been a cop, but that was it.

Jimmy left the dive shop and glanced up at the deactivated camera on the top of the fence and mumbled, "That could seriously hurt my business." He laid the bag of drugs under a white spray-painted rock on the corner of the driveway.

"All set," Jimmy said, returning to the small, thatched bungalow next to the dock where the divers continued to drink. "My guys will put it under the white rock outside in twenty minutes, and all you have to do is just replace it with the money. Simple as that."

The guy with the big head smiled. "You da' man Jimmy."

An hour later the college kids were good and drunk, they thanked Jimmy, gave him a generous tip, got their drugs from under the rock and took off. When they were out of sight down the long dirt jungle road Jimmy retrieved his money from under the white stone. Not a bad payday.

"Jimmy honey," Joni said, walking out of the building. The golden glow of the setting sun cut through the massive ferns above. "I'm going to head home. Can you lock up?"

"No prob."

"Seems like everything went well today?"

"They all left with smiles on their face."

"Sorry I snapped at you this morning."

Jimmy knew she meant it. "You kiddin' me? I deserved it."

Joni lit a cigarette and crawled into her Jeep Wrangler and said, "Yea you did Jimmy. That said, I spent most of my life being an asshole, so I guess what goes around comes around." She laughed and a cloud of smoke burst out of her mouth like a tailpipe.

Jimmy watched as the Jeep vanished down the trail.

The orange Caribbean sun continued to melt into the horizon along the Pillsbury Sound. These quiet moments were what Jimmy really loved about the Virgin Islands.

He dragged the cooler of beer in one hand and a beach chair in the other to the dock where he had the best view of the sunset. Perfect. He lit a cigarette and cracked a beer and watched the golden hue of the sun dip into darkness.

The faint sound of music and laughing was gently carried across the water with the breeze. Jimmy didn't know where it was originating from, but it appeared like someone planned on partying all night. As the sun disappeared and night began to reign Jimmy knew it was coming from the small private island in the middle of the Sound, Little Saint George.

Jimmy wondered what the gatherings were like on the island. They seemed to go on all night. He cracked another beer and lit a fresh cigarette off his old one. Lifestyles of the rich and famous. He despised them, but secretly desired to be one of the in-people: a movie star, a director, a politician. Someone with real power, not someone slowly drinking himself to death. He had dreams once, but life had taken its toll.

Like a beacon of light, Little Saint George lit up the night sky. A constant reminder of a life he'd never have. It had to be a mile away, but sitting out in the darkness it was as distant as the face of the moon. Jimmy closed his eyes and began to wonder about the strange life he'd had before he arrived on the island.

"Are you Jimmy?" a voice said behind him. The voice startled him and cut through the silence like a bullet.

Jimmy turned. A woman emerged from the darkness and walked into the moonlight. She was dressed in a black evening dress. The fragrance of perfume overpowered the odor of beer and cigarettes, which seemed to be a constant.

"Who's asking?" Jimmy replied, confused, aware of the fact that no one had ever just "shown up" at the dive shop at this time of night and alone. He questioned how many beers he had drank to make him not notice the car that had dropped her off.

"I'm Monica," the woman said, stepping into the yellow glow of the lights hanging on the bungalow. The woman wore a long sleek black dress and gold earrings. Jimmy couldn't tell her age but assumed she was much younger than she had initially seemed. A girl trying to appear as a woman.

Jimmy peered into the darkness behind her to see if there was anyone with her.

"I'm alone," she whispered. Why she whispered, Jimmy had no idea.

Jimmy ran his fingers though his hair. "Can I help you?"

Monica nodded behind him. Jimmy turned and saw the island that glowed in the darkness like the final ember of a dying fire.

The girl swallowed. "I need a ride to Little Saint George."

5

"How'd you get here?" Jimmy asked.

He had never had a request like that before. Most people traveling to Little St. George arrived on private yachts or by helicopter. To have some woman or girl just come in, and alone at that, was unusual.

"I missed my boat. A taxi in Red Hook dropped me off here. He said you could help me out."

"It's the middle of the night?"

"I have money."

"How old are you?"

"Eighteen," she said confidently.

Jimmy lit another cigarette and nodded. He doubted it, but she could be telling the truth.

"So Little Saint George, huh? Why do you want to go there?" Jimmy exhaled a haze of smoke, which was instantly carried away by the breeze. "What are you, a Governor's daughter or something?"

Something could have been many things in Jimmy's mind.

"Senator." Monica crossed her arms, clearly irritated at Jimmy's innuendo.

Jimmy had seen that look too many times in a woman before. Maybe she was telling the truth. The sun, the booze, the Caribbean, it has been known to dull one's perception of reality. "Oh yeah, which one?" he responded, attempting to repair any harm he had already done.

"Brenner." Her arms were still crossed, and her eyes fixated on Jimmy.

"I know that name," Jimmy lied. It had been quite some time since he looked at the news. He could barely name the current Vice President.

"William Brenner?" Her eyes slits of frustration.

Jimmy almost coughed up his beer as it all came back to him.

"The guy who ran for President?" Jimmy remembered him now. That was a big story, and an even bigger downfall. "He's a Senator now? I thought he was hiding in a cave somewhere? Canceled." Jimmy did feel bad about that, if he was her father.

"You're not as washed up as I thought." Monica reached into Jimmy's cooler and took out a Red Stripe. She opened the beer and took a sip. "Everyone should get a second chance. Why not him?"

Jimmy couldn't argue with her there. If anyone needed a second chance it was Jimmy, so he should have probably kept his mouth shut.

"Are you going to help me or what?" She lit a cigarette and inhaled it like she had been smoking for years—deep and slow.

Jimmy leaned backed in his cheap lawn chair. The evening was going to be more interesting than he'd thought. "I just thought you would have a helicopter or something like that?" Jimmy decided to push her buttons a little more—I mean, if you can't annoy the super-rich, what's the point?

"That's only for the President," she shot back with a "fuck you" attitude.

If she actually was the senator's daughter, then she would have to pay up like everyone else. "Well, sorry Monica, too bad your daddy lost in the primaries. I'm glad he got a second act, but no welfare cases here." Jimmy opened a new beer. The foam spilled over his hand. "It's Miller time, and I'm thirsty."

Monica marched toward Jimmy and tossed five crisp one hundred dollar bills on his lap. "If you don't want the job, I'll go find some other loser drunk with a boat to drive me over. I just thought you might need that cash. Down here, you're a dime a dozen, Jimbo."

"Jesus." Jimmy scooped up the cash on his lap. That was more money than he had made all week. "No need to be rude." Jimmy leaped to his feet and motioned toward the boat. "How did you get my name again?"

"I don't know, some loser down in Red Hook. What does it matter?"

Jimmy shrugged. "I guess it doesn't. What's going on over there, anyway? They've been partying since dusk."

Monica rolled her eyes and followed Jimmy to the boat. He helped her step from the dock to the ship so her black stilettos didn't get caught in between the wooded planks of the pier and snap off.

"I don't know," Monica said, grasping Jimmy's shoulder for balance. "A computer conference or something like that—CyberTech, CyberWorld—does it really matter?"

"I can see you're definitely not the keynote speaker."

Suddenly a silver necklace and pendant fell out of her shirt. It was a dove pendant, just like the one he'd discovered on the dive. Monica immediately put the charm back in her shirt. Like she was trying to hide it.

"I have a necklace like that."

"That's impossible," Monica replied, and promptly sat down.

Jimmy opened the glove box in front of Monica. "No, I think it's the same thing. Dove pendant? I found it diving off Little Saint George this afternoon. Pretty nice, huh?"

Jimmy held the pendant in the light of the boat so she could get a better glimpse.

"It's different," she said, without taking out her own pendant to compare. "Just some touristy piece of junk you can find in Red Hook or Charlotte Amalie."

"You're probably right." Jimmy returned it to the glove box and started the boat. They ventured toward the lone light of Little Saint George, bouncing in the darkness of the Pillsbury Sound.

"How do you like the Virgin Islands?" Jimmy said after they were thirty minutes from shore. A talker at heart, Jimmy never liked awkward silences.

"It's okay," Monica said coolly, ducking under the window to keep the wind from messing up her hair.

"Not the usual answer I get," Jimmy pried. "Typically, people say they love it here, or they never want to leave. Paradise."

"It's okay."

"This school vacation or something?" Monica was a challenging read. Probably a good poker player if she played.

"Summer break," she finally said.

After driving for twenty more minutes, Jimmy reduced the speed of the boat as they neared Little Saint George.

The island dock was dark and appeared empty, lit by only tiki torches and the pale moon above. Loudspeakers bellowed from the top of the island, where the event seemed to be taking place—a stark contrast to the tranquil, dimly lit wharf in front of the boat.

Jimmy downshifted and put the gear in neutral, guiding the vessel toward the dock. "You're pretty lucky," Jimmy said to Monica, finally breaking the silence of the ride. "I've always wanted to visit this place

—see how the ultra-rich and powerful movers and shakers live."

Monica made eye contact with Jimmy for the first time all night and said, "Trust me; it's not that special. They're just like everyone else."

"Who are you?" a deep voice announced from the dock.

Two large men walked out of the shadow and into the glow of the tiki torches. Both were well over six feet tall, with chests the size of wine barrels. One dark and clean-shaven; the other bearded and pale with a scar down his cheek. Fitted black suits showed off their hulking frames while the wires of beige earpieces disappeared under the sport coats. Probably ex-military, clearly the island muscle.

Jimmy tossed the bearded man a rope. "Can you tie me off?"

"This is a private occasion," the bearded man bellowed.

"I'm dropping the girl off," Jimmy said, sounding as if he had done this a thousand times. He wasn't the type to let some meathead goon intimidate him.

"What girl?" the clean-shaven goon ordered.

Jimmy didn't wait for permission and escorted Monica out of the boat and onto the landing.

"You on the list?" the bearded man asked Monica.

Jimmy didn't know what to say next. He hoped Monica would just run for it, or had a plan of her own.

"I'm on the list," Monica replied, stepping into the light.

"Sorry, ma'am, what's your name?" the clean-shaven man said, and scrolled through what Jimmy figured was the guest list on his phone.

"Monica Brenner," she said.

The man abruptly quit scrolling, as if he was expecting that name.

"Krauthammer," the clean-shaven man said, motioning for him to help Monica along the dock.

"Krauthammer," Jimmy said under his breath. It's not too often you see a face that perfectly fits the name, but this was one of those moments. Jimmy hopped onto the dock, not waiting for anyone to offer their hand or ask permission.

Krauthammer grabbed Jimmy's left bicep. It felt like a vice-grip. "Where are you going?" Krauthammer growled.

"Can you help me out?" Jimmy whispered to Monica, who was adjusting her hair in a pocket mirror. "I've always wanted to see what goes on here."

Monica applied some fresh lipstick and raised an eyebrow. "What do you want me to do?"

"You're not on the list, are you?" Krauthammer said again. His grip tightening, his jaw tense.

"Well, no...," Jimmy said, assuming Monica would find some way to get him in.

"Sorry," Monica shrugged and strolled across the pier toward an island pathway covered in ferns and lit by tiki torches.

"That's that, buddy. Time to go," Krauthammer said to Jimmy.

Jimmy stood his ground. "Wait, wait a minute." Jimmy hunted for an excuse. "Do you know who her father is?"

Krauthammer glanced at the other man and said, "Ramirez, do you know what he's talking about?"

Ramirez shook his head "no."

"That's the Senator's daughter," Jimmy said. Monica halted at the end of the dock as if amused, watching Jimmy suffer.

"Which Senator?" Krauthammer said.

Jimmy felt his grasp loosen and knew this was his moment. His time to do what he did best—talk.

Jimmy straightened his Hawaiian shirt. "Senator Brenner, the former Presidential candidate? Come on." Both men's faces remained blank; perhaps they were dumber than Jimmy had imagined. "You know, I'm a former cop, law enforcement, like you," Jimmy said. Typically, Jimmy preferred to lie when dealing with two idiots, but the truth came out—a fight or flight situation.

"So you're a cop, who cares?" Ramirez said.

"All I'm saying is we're on the same side. Making the island safe. I was hired to get her to the island safely. Now look at the path." Jimmy pointed at the hidden island path at the edge of the dock. Monica observed, amused as Jimmy bullshitted his way to victory. "It's pitch black, lit by torches for Christ sakes. What's this, the 1600s? She could slip and break her neck. I'm not going to take responsibility for that. I'm going to have to say —you— Hammerhead. It was your fault; you wouldn't let me walk her up the path."

"Krauthammer," he said, clearly annoyed at Jimmy mispronouncing his name.

"Krauthammer, that's what I said?"

"No, you said Hammerhead."

"Are you sure? Why would I say that?" Jimmy smirked at Monica. Idiots, Jimmy knew it.

"Fine," Krauthammer conceded. "Take her up and then come right back down. If I have to come and find you, I won't be happy."

"Of course," Jimmy said. "Fifteen minutes."

"Five minutes," Krauthammer responded, letting Jimmy pass.

"Exactly, ten minutes," Jimmy said, and gallivanted to where Monica stood at the end of the pier next to the obscure trail that led up to the island.

6

"Are you really a cop?" Monica asked as Jimmy caught up to her on the path.

Jimmy cocked his head. "Well, used to be."

"Well, you shouldn't be here." Monica's tone was serious and direct.

"That sounds like a warning." Jimmy's buzz had worn off. He knew she was serious.

"I'm not joking, dummy." Monica shook her head, "These people don't fuck around."

Jimmy lit a cigarette. "I don't know if you saw me back there with dumb and dumber, but I think I can handle myself."

Monica stopped. "Really? You think you outsmarted them?"

"What else would you call it?"

"I call it common sense. You made a good point in their mind, but right now they're calling the other idiot on steroids at the top and telling him to watch out for the guy dressed like an idiot walking Monica Brenner up the path."

"Dressed like an idiot? Me? This is my best shirt."

Monica continued up the trail. "That's the problem. This is the Caribbean, not Hawaii."

Jimmy glanced at his Hawaiian shirt. "It has palm trees; both are tropical. What's the difference?"

"And you smell like cigarettes and beer."

Jimmy sniffed his shirt and shrugged. "That's the tiki torch fumes you're smelling. Highly flammable."

"Yea right—just don't breathe on the flames. You'll blow up the island."

"Can we stop for a sec? I'm a little winded. It's been a while since—"

"—since you got any exercise?" Monica shot back, annoyed now. "We're almost there."

The voice over the louder speaker became clearer as they neared the top of the path.

The thick island ferns that engulfed the path opened up like a massive theater curtain to reveal a Greek-style amphitheater. Two to three hundred people sat row by row in a half-circle that looked down on a stage where a woman dressed in a conservative grey suit addressed the audience.

Jimmy did feel underdressed when viewing the crowd sipping expensive wine and eating shrimp cocktail delivered in crystal bowls from black-bowtie-wearing waiters buzzing around like flies.

The men in attendance wore tuxedos and expensive watches; the ladies looked their best with evening gowns and jewels—the more revealing outfits differed on age, as did the Botox, facelifts, and hair extensions.

Mixed in with the tuxedos were military uniforms from around the world, decorated in medals and badges. Jimmy noticed the Union Jack on one sleeve, the Canadian Maple Leaf on the other, the Australian or New Zealand flag on the other—he could never tell the difference.

Monica was right. Jimmy clearly didn't belong here.

He took some relief in the fact that he was behind the crowd, in the back of the amphitheater with the dark jungle ferns behind him. No one would know he was there unless they turned around, and that was unlikely.

Jimmy stepped forward and peered over the backs of the crowd to get a better view of the woman speaking. She stood at the base of the concrete amphitheater on a slab of granite and seemed to have the whole audience hanging on every word.

Jimmy didn't recognize her, but he thought she must be significant to fascinate this audience. Behind the woman was a large poster that read "Cyber Talks" in a futuristic font that reminded him of *Star Trek*.

The woman's voice echoed out of the loudspeakers above. "That's why, with the support of the people in this theater," the woman spoke into the small mic headset with a passion that looked over-rehearsed, like a politician, "I believe together, we can rid the internet of hate speech and hurtful ideas that are destroying our children. Social media and the internet needs to be free of hurtful, racist, and sexist ideas. The radical right has found its voice, and we need to combat it and make sure the internet is free of hateful and xenophobic ideas. That's why tonight I propose and ask for your support in helping me get the Internet Freedom Act passed."

The crowd erupted into applause.

"I knew it," Jimmy said to himself, flipping a cigarette into his lips. "Another fuckin' politician trying to save us from ourselves."

"Monica," Jimmy turned to his right, expecting to see the young woman, but she was gone.

Figures, he thought.

"Sir," one of the tuxedo-wearing ants said as he rushed over to Jimmy. "You can't smoke in here."

"Of course not. We're outside." Jimmy licked the tips of his fingers and pinched out the ember of the cigarette and put it into his breast pocket and said, "A treat for later."

Jimmy grabbed two glasses of champagne from the waiter's tray before the waiter left in disgust.

Jimmy slugged one glass down and then sipped on the other with his pinky up and looking refined. He watched as the military man with the Union Jack on his uniform approached him. Jimmy assumed the man was a general or navy commander; he stopped, smirked, and looked Jimmy up and down before continuing on his way.

"Sorry your highness, I didn't get the memo."

"Without further ado," the woman at the front of the amphitheater continued, "I am proud to introduce my colleague, former Presidential candidate and now Senator from the commonwealth of Virginia, William Brenner."

The crowd applauded again. Jimmy wanted to choke. He hated these types of superficial events.

William Brenner strutted onto the stage, tall and lanky; his suit was a size too big. White frosted his hair at the temples, while the rest was noticeably dyed jet-black. Jimmy vaguely remembered Brenner's election, but who could forget how it crashed and burned into a blaze of gambling and hookers—all the things that typical politicians do. Still, he just didn't have the charisma to pull it off like some others.

Brenner looked older, weathered, one could say. The years and stress had taken their toll. Bags under his eyes, teeth no longer that ultra-bright white that so many public figures have.

William Brenner adjusted his suit, an instinctive move that harkened back to when he was the new political savior coming to deliver the party from evil. Like so many do, he'd believed his own hype. He'd thought he was untouchable.

"I would first like to thank Congresswoman Reilly for her informative speech," Brenner's voice cracked into the microphone. "I would also like to thank our gracious host Jonathan Alderman for putting on this occasion." His words were flat and clear to the audience watching.

Brenner coughed and licked his lips as if preparing to make a statement that went off-script. "First, I would like to pledge my steadfast commitment to the freedom and openness of the internet."

Jimmy yawned and caught himself staring at the breast of a trophy wife sitting next to a fat, sweaty man.

"But I'm afraid the Internet Freedom Act is just a nice name." Brenner now spoke with a level of passion that was not in his earlier comments. "Like the Patriot Act before it—something that had good intentions, but in fact was a smokescreen to hide the truth from people. Power."

Boos filled the amphitheater.

Brenner spoke louder: "How can you not see that this act aims to censor and control speech? If you censor one type of speech, you censor it all."

The boos grew louder, causing Jimmy to pay attention again. How could he not admire someone who stood in front of an audience of people booing him?

Congresswoman Reilly mouthed, *What are you doing, William?* from the side of the stage.

Brenner ignored her.

"This is all about control," his voice roared. "What gives us the power to control the words of others? It's against the very fabric of what this country stands for."

Brenner's microphone abruptly cut off. He continued to speak, but Jimmy couldn't hear what he was saying over the angry audience.

Suddenly Jimmy felt a hand on his shoulder. Krauthammer stood behind him. His bearded face contorted in a scowl.

"Let's go." Krauthammer ground his teeth.

"Oh, it's you." Jimmy tried to turn on his charm. "I was just coming down to see you."

"Let's go. Now." Krauthammer squeezed Jimmy's shoulder.

Jimmy winced. "Yea, Yea, yea. The speech was boring anyway. Too much talk. You know, politics and stuff."

Jimmy knew Krauthammer wasn't buying any of it. He just hoped he was still going to leave with all his teeth still in place. Jimmy imagined Krauthammer's great grandfather crushing skulls during World War II and thought that bloodlust had to have been passed down through the generations.

Jimmy played it cool and let Krauthammer escort him back to the island trail that lead down to the boat. Jimmy took one final scan of the theater to see where Monica had run off to. He saw her on the other side of the theater. She was passionately talking to a girl. She seemed agitated about something. Scared. Jimmy noticed the girl Monica was speaking to had a pink streak in her hair. She wore a white polo shirt like she was one of the island employees.

Something seemed off. Something was wrong.

"Wait," Jimmy said to Krauthammer.

"Not a chance." Krauthammer squeezed Jimmy hard, now dragging him toward the path.

As Jimmy exited the amphitheater, he observed the girl with the streak in her hair nod in Brenner's direction.

Senator William Brenner appeared distressed and beaten as he walked toward the two girls. Something was clearly wrong.

Jimmy felt what resembled a train plunging into his stomach as Krauthammer punched him. The next thing Jimmy knew, he was gasping for air and being yanked down the hidden island path.

By the time Jimmy caught his breath, he was at the pier. The smell of salt water mixed with tiki-torch fuel woke him right up. At the dock's edge, Krauthammer gave Jimmy one final thrust, and Jimmy fell into the boat. He tumbled on to the driver's seat, kinking his back in the process.

"What the fuck, man?" Jimmy panted, rubbing his back where he fell against the chair.

Ramirez untied the boat lines, then planted his wing-tipped shoes against the boat and shoved it into open water.

"Self-defense," Krauthammer chuckled.

"I can attest to that," Ramirez added. "Bye-bye.

"Yea, well, your party sucked anyway," Jimmy shouted.

He turned on the engine and headed back toward St. Thomas. The image of Senator William Brenner walking toward those two frightened girls burned into his mind. Their hollow and defeated eyes reminded Jimmy Walsh of a past he never wanted to visit again.

7

Marooned was a local bar just past the sleepy down-town of touristy Red Hook. A dive bar truly accessible only by boat. Jimmy went straight there from Little Saint George. He replayed the whole night in his head as the vessel cruised by the boat graveyard that lined the dark shore, where every piece of junk leftover from the numerous hurricanes that hit St. Thomas over the years seemed to have collected.

Jimmy didn't think much about Ramirez and Krauthammer, two people he gladly would watch drown if he had the chance. But he thought about Monica and the girl with the pink streak in her hair. Something seemed off between the two. They seemed like friends, but why would a Senator's daughter know someone on the island? It's certainly possible, but how often is Cinderella friends with the person who mops the floors?

Jimmy slowed the boat down and hugged the shoreline. It didn't matter anyway. He would never see them again. Large broken masses from sailboats rotting in the boat graveyard sent jagged shards of moonlight across the water. His mind turned to how long it would be before the dive boat ended up there.

Suddenly a spotlight from ahead turned on, blasting Jimmy with white light. He squinted and raised his arm to block the beam, which felt like a supernova in his eyes. A police siren sounded for a second.

Shit, he thought. If a cop wanted to be a prick and give him a hard time, he would lose his license for sure. There was no way he would pass a breathalyzer even if he had lost his buzz from earlier.

The floodlight abruptly shut off. Jimmy's eyes tried to adjust back to the night, but all he saw were color spots. He was still blind.

"Jimbo," he heard the Caribbean accent of the police officer say over a loudspeaker.

Jimmy knew that voice and was instantly on edge. He shouted, "I still can't see, so don't blame me if I crash into you."

He knew the boat and voice belonged to Ajax Cason, a local island cop Jimmy had seen around over the years. He must have been 240lbs and always busted Jimmy's balls. Originally from St. Croix, Cason came over to St. Thomas because "that's where all the action is," he had told Jimmy once.

"You walkin' home dis time, right Jimbo?" Cason called from his boat.

"I'm just going for the fried shrimp." Jimmy wasn't technically lying. The last time Jimmy visited Marooned, he passed out at the bar. When he woke up, he told everyone he was giving up drinking. He did for a while, but who was he kiddin'? You don't get sober in the Caribbean.

"Dhat right?" Cason said, the boats now close enough to talk. Jimmy's eyes returned to normal. He knew Cason didn't believe him, but so what? He didn't need to know.

"Just be careful, man." Cason grinned and accelerated the throttle on his high-speed police boat and took off into the darkness.

The glow of Christmas lights coiled around the bar, which lay down a long splintered dock, guided Jimmy in. He threw the ropes to Eddie, who sat at the end of the pier in a beach chair.

"How you doin' Jimmy?" Eddie said, wrapping the lines around the dock moorings.

"Be better soon once I have that drink. I'll tell you that much. Cason was just bustin' my balls."

At sixteen years old, Eddie was a good kid and a good worker. He had worked at Marooned as long as he could remember and reminded Jimmy of himself when he was that age. A little bit of a rebel, but with common sense.

"I haven't seen you in a while," Eddie said. "What you been up to?"

"Drinking," Jimmy responded with his usual no-apology mentality.

"Sobriety didn't last long, huh?"

"You know how it is; what's life without its vices? How's Kate?"

"The same. She's not dating anyone if that's what you're asking." Eddie leaned in.

"Really? I heard otherwise."

"She said that he was just a rebound. You know, some rich tourist or something like that."

Jimmy turned off the boat with a snap and exhaled, "Honestly, I wish you didn't tell me that. Not the kind of image I want rolling around in my head."

"You asked."

"Not really."

"Jimmy, you have a smoke?"

Jimmy reached into his breast and pulled out a joint. "It's half-cooked, but it's Curtis's brew, so it should do the trick."

"I owe you." Eddie lit the joint.

Jimmy tossed Eddie the boat keys. "Listen to the radio if you want, just don't let me drive home. It might be one of those nights."

Jimmy made his way along the deteriorating narrow dock. The red and green glow of the Christmas lights and the sound of "Three Little Birds" by Bob Marley guided his way.

The closer Jimmy grew to the bar, the more comfortable he felt. The events of the night melted away. He was happy that Kate was single, but still couldn't get the rich tourist out of his mind. It didn't matter; it was his fault they broke up anyway.

Marooned sat in the jungle ferns about thirty feet from where the water met land. A good choice, because the dock area stank of boat fuel and rotting fish. Jimmy lit a cigarette to kill the smell and stepped under the thatched roof and into the glow of the Christmas lights.

"What's up, fellas? Jimmy's back. Let the party begin." Jimmy moved past the plastic chairs and tables scattered across the concrete slab floor toward the saltwater-weather wooden barstools hugging the bar.

Nothing had changed since he had been there last. Nautical memorabilia hung above the bar. Christmas lights snaked around old compasses and steering wheels.

The deadbeat locals were all the same, still in varying stages of alcoholism. Jimmy nodded to Harris, a regular who resembled an old pirate, a dirty beard and yellow teeth. All he needed was an eyepatch to sell it, and he could have a gig in downtown Red Hook with a cup for change. Tourists would gladly take pictures and throw money in.

"Jimmy," Harris scowled, "You haven't been around in a while. I was hoping you got the bends on one of your stupid dives, and your head exploded."

"Only after I come up after going down on your wife." A few of the other drunks laughed in the back. Harris returned to his plastic cup of cheap rum.

"Jimmy Walsh" a familiar voice said from the other side of the bar.

Kate Pellbrook popped her head up from retrieving a new bottle of Titos from underneath the bar. "I see you haven't lost your sense of humor."

Kate crossed her arms. He hair pulled back into a bun, her skin like dark chocolate. She still look as beautiful as ever in her sleeveless Rolling Stones shirt. That was always Jimmy's favorite shit. The massive red lips spread out across her breasts, accentuating their fullness.

"Hi Kate," Jimmy said.

Jimmy didn't know if she was going to hit him over the head with the bottle or pour him a drink. They had a long history and a lot of good times too. Jimmy had been in the Virgin Islands seven years now, two of them with her.

"You going to sit down," Kate raised an eyebrow, "or you just gonna stand there?"

Jimmy moved toward the bar.

"It's been a while."

Kate grabbed a rag and wiped a bar spot clean for Jimmy and said, "Thought you stopped drinking?"

"I did, but now I started again," Jimmy said proudly.

"I think you set a record." Kate poured a shot of Titos in front of Jimmy.

Jimmy glanced back to see if he still had the full attention of the barroom.

"I am quite a catch." Jimmy reached for the shot, but Kate grabbed it first.

"Nah, I'd throw you back." Kate gulped the shot, and the whole bar burst into laughter.

"Amen to that," Harris belched, barely able to get his words out.

"Tough crowd." Jimmy put a crisp one hundred dollar bill on the bar then addressed the whole bar-room. "I guess I'm not buying anyone a shot tonight."

"Really?" Kate wasn't impressed. "You still have an unpaid tab from before your stint on the wagon."

"I know, I haven't forgotten," Jimmy said defensively, and slid two hundred dollar bills across the bar.

Kate pocketed the cash. "Big day?"

"Something like that."

"Well, Mr. Big Day, you sure you want to buy all of them a drink?"

"Everyone except Harris."

"Fuck you, Jimmy," Harris mumbled.

"Oh, sorry, did I say that out loud?" Jimmy chuckled and then locked eyes with Kate. For a moment, all their history bubbled to the surface. He bit his lip. Jimmy was sorry for all the pain he caused her. The days he would go without talking to her; unanswered phone calls and texts. Being on and off.

"Pour yourself a drink too," Jimmy said, clasping her hand like he used to.

"Jimmy," her eyes watered, "that ship has sailed." She pulled her hand away and turned before the tear fell, "but I will take the drink," she said with her back toward him.

Jimmy knew he deserved that, but there was nothing he could do. He still had feelings for Kate.

"So you going to tell me where you got that big payday from?" Kate said, preparing the shots.

"Remember that guy Brenner who ran for President a few years back?"

"His wife caught him screwing the babysitter," Harris mumbled while he and the others approached the bar to retrieve their free shot.

"Is he having a shot too?" Kate asked Jimmy, glancing at Harris.

"Of course I am, Kate. This son-of-a-bitch owes me more than a cheap shot of whiskey."

Jimmy nodded. "He can have a shot."

"I remember when that story broke." Kate added another shot to the tray and gave Jimmy a Red Stripe.

Jimmy popped the top off like he did a thousand times and threw it at the trash. Miss.

"Anyway, I was just sitting there on the dock watching the sun go down, and his daughter threw down some cash and asked me to give her a lift to Little Saint George."

"Little Saint George," Kate said. "Really?" The whole barroom was now interested in his story. "What was it like?"

"Exactly what you think," Jimmy and the rest drank their shot, "a bunch of rich people playing god with all the rest of us."

Harris wiped the drool from his beard and scowled. "I wouldn't have taken their money. I'll tell you that much."

Jimmy raised an eyebrow. "But you'll take a drink that's bought with their money?"

"Well, that's a different story," Harris laughed. "A drunk knows to keep his mouth shut if he wants free booze."

Jimmy motioned to Kate for another round.

"There's no middle ground with you, is there? All or nothing, stop or go?"

"This is a bar, isn't it?" Jimmy knew there was a part of Kate that still worried about him. That desired him to get better. To eventually let go of the demons he carried everywhere he went.

The night had been rough.

His stomach still ached from where Krauthammer punched him. Jimmy thought of Monica and the girl with the pink hair. Their look frightened him and made him have glimpses into the past he had tried to bury. All those years ago, the pain, the hatred, all rose to the surface. The events that drove him to this little piece of paradise at the edge of the world were clawing back. His little utopia, he liked to call it, where he couldn't be affected by the outside world, was breaking down, shattering.

Jimmy downed another shot and knew only one thing: he didn't want to be alone. Kate was the closest thing he had to a friend.

8

YEARS EARLIER.

James Walsh Balzano, wearing his best suit, stepped out of the Boston Municipal Courthouse with his lawyer Lauren D. Farendetti into the cold January sun. The air was fresh, directly the opposite of sitting in a stale courtroom for three hours. It was hard to believe he was here defending himself. After ten years on the force, he never imagined he would have ended up in this position.

Jimmy rounded the concrete wall of the courthouse to barrages of screams and hostile faces. There must have been twenty or thirty people. A man spat on him, and another shrieked something incoherent. Many held signs and chanted, but all of it was a white noise of contorted angry faces.

Jimmy wanted to tell them it wasn't his fault. He wasn't responsible, but he knew you couldn't reason with a mob once they had their pitchforks. They wanted blood, his blood, and they were willing to do anything to get it.

Lauren D. Farendetti held Jimmy by the arm of his blue peacoat while four Boston police officers escorted them through the crowd. Jimmy squinted and clenched his jaw, trying his best to pretend it didn't bother him. Farendetti's support was reassuring, but from the twitch of her arm, he understood she craved to get as far away from this, from him as possible.

The mob was so close he could feel the warm, wet breath of people screaming obscenities at him. Their scent was palpable, like a fire waiting for the gasoline.

"Pig!" a young woman shouted as she waved a homemade peace sign.

Another young man pointed his finger at Jimmy and yelled, "Piece of shit, rat cop! Fuck you. You should have died."

Suddenly a black town car screeched to a halt just beyond the protesters. That was their exit, and Jimmy wanted to get there as swiftly as possible.

The police officers pushed through the crowd like a snowplow, and Farendetti quickly opened the black town car's back door.

Suddenly, Jimmy felt something hit him in the back of the head. He winced in pain. It was hard. A bottle, a can, maybe? He glanced up to see who had thrown it, but it was impossible to know. Judging by the anger of the crowd, it could have been anyone.

"Jimmy, get in. It's not safe," Farendetti shouted. Her voice was stern and severe, far different from her usual calm demeanor.

Another object launched from the crowd hit him. Not bothering to look, Jimmy promptly got into the vehicle, quickly followed by Farendetti. One of the officers closed the doors behind her. Jimmy made eye contact with the officer. A cold, hard stare greeted Jimmy. At that moment, he knew he was all alone. If it wasn't for those officers' badges, he believed they would have fed him to the wolves or even been wolves themselves.

Jimmy shielded his eyes and turned away from the window, then let out a large gasp once. He gradually lifted his head, the weight of the past few days squarely on his back. His neck still hurt from the bottle or whatever was thrown at him. However, everything melted away when he saw his girlfriend, Hayley Diaz, in front of him.

She looked beautiful in her tan coat and sunglasses --the type Jackie Kennedy or Audrey Hepburn wore. He wanted to grab her, hug her, and tell her how much he loved her. Her support was everything to him. But he wanted to give her time. Jimmy could tell she was disturbed by the protesters banging on the car's window as it drove away. Time, he thought. Just give her time.

Hayley's silence unnerved Jimmy. What was she thinking? Was she angry at him? Did she still love him?

Once the car cleared the protesters and turned onto the road, Hayley jumped to his side of the vehicle. She embraced him and offered her support. Jimmy buried his face in her shoulders and wanted to cry but couldn't. He wouldn't let himself do that.

"It's all going to be okay," Hayley said. "This will all be over soon, James."

Jimmy gazed up and beamed. He couldn't believe how lucky he was to have a girl like this. Most women would have fled right when things went wrong, but not Hayley. She had been with him through it all.

Lauren Farendetti cleared her throat and put her briefcase on her lap. She adjusted her papers so as to signal: this wasn't over yet.

"James," Farendetti said. "Today was just the beginning."

Jimmy pulled Hayley closer and glanced out the rear window. Gathered outside the courthouse, the protesters were still chanting as if they had no intention of leaving. Jimmy recognized the worst was yet to come.

Jimmy and Hayley returned to their apartment twenty minutes later. The first thing Jimmy did was open a bottle of Pinot Grigio from the wine fridge and pour two glasses. He couldn't stop shaking. He needed something to take the edge off. Something light and smooth.

Jimmy handed Hayley the second glass, but she refused.

It was apparent the process had taken a toll on Hayley. She might have acted tough in the courtroom and on the car ride, but Jimmy wasn't sure how she truly felt.

Hayley began to weep.

Jimmy gently put his glass down and reassured her. "I'm sorry, babe. I know this has been hard on you too. You've been there every step of the way. I love you so much. I want to let you know how much you mean to me."

Hayley raised her head and stared Jimmy in the eyes. "It's been so hard. The things that they are calling you. It's terrible, James."

"I'm sorry. It will be over soon. I know it will. We can start over again. Somewhere warm." He attempted to make a joke. "Florida?"

"I just don't know if I can do it anymore." Hayley wiped her eyes. "Every day is worse than the next."

Jimmy understood. He placed the hair that had fallen in front of her eyes behind her ear. "Stay home tomorrow," he pleaded. "You've been at the courthouse every other day. Stay home tomorrow. Relax. We can meet up after."

"It's not that." Hayley backed away. "I don't know if I can do this—you and me anymore."

"What do you mean?" Jimmy didn't understand. Maybe he'd misheard her. "You and I?"

"This. You and I. Everyone at work knows who you are, James. They know what happened. They see my face right next to yours on the news. My family asks questions. It will never end. YouTube, the internet—this will follow you and me everywhere. And James—Florida?" Jimmy sensed anger in her voice, "I don't want to move. Why would you even say that?"

Jimmy couldn't believe what he was hearing. "But what about marriage? A family? Everything we talked about?"

Hayley took a deep breath and said, "James, after what you did, I don't want you to ever be the father of my children. Ever."

9

The morning after Jimmy Walsh's night at Marooned, he woke to a cooler of ice water dumped on his head. He flailed in all directions like a freshly caught tuna and slid off his beach chair onto the hard wooden dock.

"What the fuck?" Jimmy howled.

Confusion struck him as he tried to get his bearings. His head throbbed, his vision was blurry, his eyes burned from the blaze of the morning sun blasting through the tree fern tops. Tequila, beer, and cigarettes were still on his tongue.

Jimmy replayed the events of the previous night, working backward from when it all went hazy. He recalled chatting with Kate, although not what about. Fingers crossed he didn't say anything too outrageous. Little Saint George suddenly flickered across his beer-battered brain, followed by Krauthammer, Senator Brenner, the girl with the pink streak in her hair, and then there was Monica Brenner, the young, stunning, daughter of a US senator, seemingly indifferent to it all. Except at the end, Jimmy thought. He remembered her worried, detached gaze as she spoke to the girl with the pink hair.

"Jimmy," a voice said. His hearing muffled from the hangover; he assumed it came from the asshole who had dumped the cooler on his head.

Jimmy opened his eyes, or at least tried to. He reached for his sunglasses, which never left the nylon strap around his neck.

His vision sharpened. He was back at the Dive Shop. Joni stood over him, more than a little concerned.

"Jimmy," Joni lowered her voice, seeming to realize her method of waking someone up was a bit medieval. "We got divers coming. They'll be here any minute."

"I'm up. I'm up." Jimmy gradually got to his feet. "You almost gave me a fuckin' heart attack."

"You're going to give yourself a heart attack."

Jimmy studied the dive boat. Not a scratch on it—or no more than the usual. He was relieved he didn't crash it on his way back. Kill himself or someone else.

"Right now, you're thinking, 'how the hell did I get back here'?" Joni said.

Jimmy nodded. "That had crossed my mind."

"The kid from the bar dropped you off this morning. What do they say? 'God protects drunks and kids'?"

Jimmy wondered about that. He was glad the boat was in one piece, but his noggin felt like fruit in a blender. His stomach stung from where Krauthammer had punched him. Jimmy wanted to vomit, but that could have been the booze too.

Jimmy chugged the remaining water from the cooler that Joni had half-emptied on his head and tried hydrate, then he immediately fell back into the beach chair.

"Can I get five minutes?" Jimmy pleaded.

"Brought you the paper." Joni tossed Jimmy the local newspaper.

His head still hurt. "I don't think I can read right now."

Suddenly a helicopter buzzed by overhead, drawing Jimmy and Joni's attention to the serene Caribbean Sea.

"What's going on out there?" Jimmy squinted.

The helicopter hovered above what appeared to be two police boats anchored in the Sound. Divers were in the water, and it seemed they were searching for something.

Indifferent to what was happening in the water, Joni said, "How should I know?"

Jimmy carefully walked over to the boat and reached his hand through the window, grabbing binoculars from the dashboard.

He moved to the end of the splintery wooden dock and dropped his sunglasses around his neck. Jimmy squinted one more time as if to wish away the hangover that still pulsated in his head. He placed the binoculars to his eyes and couldn't believe what he observed.

A body was in the process of being removed from the water. Jimmy couldn't tell who it was, male or female. But he knew one thing for sure. It was dead.

A taxi pulled onto the Dive Shop property, its tires crunching against the stones and seashells that made up the driveway. A family of four leaped out: mother and father were in their early fifties, their kids, a boy and a girl, both around twenty. The typical American family, Jimmy thought. They probably had a dog and picket fence back home in the suburbs.

Suddenly Joni slapped the dive boat keys against Jimmy's chest. "It's showtime."

Thirty minutes later, the dive boat cruised across the Pillsbury Sound. The fresh air sobered Jimmy up a bit. There were no plans for a new dive location today, plus the World War II wreck was always a knockout, and the spot would get him a better glimpse at what the cops were doing.

The family was pleasant. The father tried his best to appease the family by enthusiastically giving a scuba refresher to his son and daughter, who remained buried in their phones. His wife sunned on the deck of the boat and polished off her second glass of rum punch—the perfect tourists for a hangover. No small talk, and Jimmy knew they would tip well. Plus, he had other things on his mind: the dead body.

The police boats were roughly three hundred yards off the shoreline of Little Saint George. It was apparent the body had to have had come from the island. Jimmy steered the vessel near the police boats and hoped the tourists wouldn't object.

"What's going on over there?" the father asked, appearing just as curious as Jimmy.

"Don't know. Let me see if I can get a little closer."

Jimmy was relieved the father didn't mind the deviation.

Minutes later, Jimmy noticed Officer Cason was piloting one of the boats. His bulky frame nearly took up the whole cockpit of the ship. Jimmy pulled up next to him. "What's going on?"

"Sorry, Jimbo," Cason said with his Caribbean charm, "Glad you made it back alive from last night, but you gonna have to find a new place to dive today."

Jimmy leaned in and lowered his voice so the family couldn't hear. "Saw you pull someone from the water earlier?" He thought of Monica and the girl with the pink streak in her hair.

Jimmy could tell from the way Cason cocked his head he didn't want to part with the information.

"Come on," Jimmy pried. "It's gonna be in the newspaper anyway."

"You have a way with words." Cason took off his police cap and ran his hand over the top of his head. "You know William Brenner?"

"Yea, I heard of him."

"Well, even Senators can't breathe underwater."

10

Later that day, Jimmy was relieved when the tourists finally left. The dive went perfectly: the dad got to look cool in front of his kids, and the mom got hammered in the sun while she read a novel about banging the pool boy. Jimmy didn't know for sure, but that's what the book cover looked like. In the end, everyone was happy, and they left him with a generous tip.

Jimmy relished this time of day. The dive shop was quiet, and he had no responsibilities. The sunset across the Pillsbury Sound cast the whole island in a warm caramel glow. Jimmy pulled a fistful of ice from the cooler, dumped it in a plastic cup, and grabbed the bottle of Captain Morgan's rum behind the makeshift bar of the bungalow.

Joni shuffled out of the shadowy concrete building. "Want one?" Jimmy asked, then turned his focus back to making his cocktail.

"I'm all set, Jimmy," Joni replied.

"More for me," Jimmy chuckled to himself, "I found out what all that commotion was about."

"Jimmy," Joni cut him off, attempting to draw his attention, but Jimmy was too busy preparing his drink.

"Senator drowned. One less politician." Jimmy shrugged, then started to sing as he stirred his drink. "Another One Bites the Dust, duh, duh, duh. Another One Bites the Dust."

"Jimmy!" Joni spoke in a tone that reminded Jimmy of his mother.

Jimmy abruptly froze and hesitantly turned around while taking a sip of his beverage.

Next to Joni stood a woman dressed in a sleek navy-blue dress. She seemed oddly familiar, but Jimmy couldn't place her. Had he met her before? A brunette, maybe ten years or so older than him. The years had been generous to her, a lot more merciful than they had been to him. She was gorgeous.

"Jimmy," Joni said again. This time softer and pleasant. "I would like to introduce you to Mrs. Brenner, the Senator's wife."

Jimmy gulped hard and searched for words and excuses. "Um... I'm sorry. I didn't mean to say that." His eyes darted back to Joni and then to Mrs. Brenner. "This is my second, no, third drink."

"Would it have mattered?" Mrs. Brenner asked bluntly.

Jimmy glanced to Joni for aid.

"I'll be in my office," Joni said promptly before abruptly leaving the two of them alone.

"Mr. Walsh," Mrs. Brenner said once Joni was out of earshot.

"Jimmy, please." Jimmy attempted to press reset on his first impression. "I'm so sorry for your loss, Mrs. Brenner. Could I make you a cocktail? A rum punch?" Once the words left his lips, he felt like a peasant for saying them. She wasn't the type who drank from a plastic cup. She was nearly the first lady of the United States.

"I'll make this brief," she said, taking charge of the conversation. "There was a girl here last night, correct?"

"Yes. Your daughter. I drove her to the island."

Mrs. Brenner cocked her head, like a lawyer for the prosecution, and said, "Is that what she told you?"

"That's right," Jimmy answered like he was in court all over again.

"Well, Mr. Walsh, you see, I'm Senator Brenner's wife, and we don't have a daughter."

Confusion struck Jimmy like the freezing bucket of water Joni had thrown on him earlier.

"Okay?" Jimmy answered as if asking a question. What did she have to do with him anyway?

"Who was the girl?" Mrs. Brenner said.

"Um...how should I know?"

"Look, Mr. Walsh," Mrs. Brenner snapped. "I don't know what type of sick business you run here, but this is deplorable."

Mrs. Brenner approached Jimmy and handed him a photo. The picture was blurry, but Jimmy could tell it was of him and Monica arriving at the Little Saint George island dock—probably from a security camera.

"What is this?" Jimmy said defensively. "I told you I drove her there."

Mrs. Brenner's eyes started to water, and then she blurted out, "What do you do, bring girls over every night?"

"Wait a minute, lady," Jimmy said, setting down his drink. "What do you think I am, some pimp? I won't have you running around and smearing my name. The girl showed up here, asking for a ride. She said she missed the boat. She said she was your daughter. She had money. She was on the guest list for Christ's sakes."

"I'm going to get to the bottom of this. My husband has powerful friends."

Jimmy took the statement as a warning. He swallowed and said clearly, "I know exactly who your husband is, and I bet he has powerful friends. But, and I'm sorry I have to say this, this isn't the first time he got mixed up in a scandal, so don't blame me."

"That's a private matter," she said.

Jimmy's defense seemed to cause her to backtrack, which provided him some relief from the accusation. "I just wanted to know," she added, "where is the girl?"

"I don't know where she is or who she is," Jimmy retreated to the bar and made another drink. "Beyond the boat ride, it doesn't involve me."

Mrs. Brenner stepped out of the shadow. Jimmy could tell she was in distress. Her voice cracked. "Do you think she's local?" Her voice was softer, gentler, almost as if she regretted her earlier tone.

"I've never seen her before."

"If she was local, would you be able to find somebody like that?"

Jimmy understood the implication, but wanted her to clarify. "What do you mean, 'like that'?"

"You know—escorts?" Mrs. Brenner was apprehensive about addressing the topic.

"What? Do you think I know every lowlife on St. Thomas?"

Jimmy felt her judgment as her eyes leapt from the decaying boat under the palm trees to the half drank rum bottle and scattered beer cans on the ground.

"You might have a few ideas," she bit her lip, doing her best to hide her opinion, but it was apparent. "There are people in that line of work on this island, right?"

"Obviously," Jimmy said bluntly. "This is the human race we're talking about. Those people exist everywhere."

"Could you ask around?"

"Me? You got the wrong idea, Mrs. Brenner. Ask the police."

"I can't go through another front-page scandal about my husband's infidelity. It ruined me once. I can't go through it again. You know the island better than anyone."

Jimmy understood her desire to keep this private. He had gone through hell being a tabloid sensation himself before he had escaped to paradise. However, this was over his head.

"I'm sorry," he said regrettably. "There's nothing I can do."

"I'll pay," she said confidently. "A thousand dollars a day."

Jimmy almost choked on his drink. "Let me see that photo again."

Mrs. Brenner handed him the photo.

"This the best photo you have of her?"

"I want to keep this very quiet."

Jimmy was in. If this went on long enough, he could eventually buy his own boat and start Jimmy's Dive Shop. "Do you think she had something to do with his death?"

"I don't know, but she was the last person to see William alive."

11

The next day Jimmy woke up early. The thousand dollars in ten crisp, clean one hundred dollar bills that Lisa Brenner had dropped in his lap felt like a warm blanket. Jimmy hadn't held that much cash in years.

Having no clients that day, Jimmy decided to take it easy: he scrubbed the boat, cleaned the windows, changed the oil. It wasn't until dusk when his real plans for the day began.

Jimmy yanked a rain tarp off his moped. A sky-blue Vespa SXL he kept hidden behind a palm tree. An older model with a few dents and scratches Jimmy purchased second-hand from a rental shop. It operated fine for the amount of time he drove it.

Jimmy lit a cigarette, then drove onto the dirt road like riding a Harley, pulling out of a biker bar. Ten minutes later, he was on the main road. Still cracked and eroded from the off-season storms, Jimmy made sure to stay away from the edges. Even after seven years of living on St. Thomas, he was still getting used to driving on the opposite side of the road like the British.

Downtown Red Hook was beginning to come alive for the night. A sunburned tourist walked into a restaurant for a nice dinner while others stumbled out of the ferry terminal with drinks still in their hands, probably coming back from St. John Island.

Red Hook was no Charlotte Amalie, the US Virgin Islands' capital city located on the other side of St. Thomas, but Red Hook was still hoping for the tourists who liked to take it a little slower. Jimmy sped through downtown, and before he knew it, he passed the boat graveyard. Broken ship masses cast shadows like headstones on the road in front of him.

He thought of Kate as he passed the small dirt path, the only road access that brought you to Marooned. He still missed her, or what they once had.

Twenty minutes later, he was driving through the dark hills of St. Thomas. Large deteriorating Danish West Indie style houses built centuries ago scattered the side of the road. Jimmy abruptly came upon a dark driveway, one of those old houses, and he pulled in.

"It's Jimmy," he shouted into the intercom on the side of the large iron gate.

Moments later, he heard a buzz, then the grinding of metal as the gate slid open. To the right of the entrance was a cage of three mean-looking Pitbulls. No matter how many times Jimmy visited, those dogs always scared the shit out of him. They howled and drooled. Jimmy was sure they would tear a person apart if they had to.

"Shut up," a voice shouted from inside the house. A silhouetted figure emerged. Jimmy parked the moped, and the gate shut behind him.

Curtis Blue stepped into the moonlight and greeted Jimmy with a massive smile. "Jimbo, how's life by dah see, mon?"

"Interesting, that's for sure," Jimmy said with a smirk and got off his moped. The two men embraced each other like old friends.

Curtis Blue was a successful local business owner who had a few properties he leased to tourist-friendly restaurants in Red Hook. A skinny man with massive dreadlocks down his back, he was never without a smile. He was one of Jimmy's oldest friends on the island.

Minutes later, they were walking through Curtis's house. Jimmy said "hi" to Curtis's wife as she prepared dinner in the kitchen. She smiled back. Curtis's son played video games in the living room, indifferent to Jimmy. Curtis escorted Jimmy out onto the deck where they would have some privacy to talk.

The extensive hillside deck spanned the house's width and stood fifty feet above the ground on massive pillars.

"I never get sick of this view." Jimmy gazed over the jungle hillside. In the distance, he could see Charlotte Amilee lit up like a Christmas Tree. A massive Royal Caribbean cruise ship, almost as big as the city itself, docked in the deepwater port once used for US submarines during the Second World War.

Curtis popped the top off a Red Stripe and passed it to Jimmy. Even though the Caribbean cooled off nice at night, a cold beer always tasted good.

"You hear about that Senator that drowned over off Little Saint George?" Jimmy asked.

Curtis pulled out a briefcase filled with small bags of powder and pills, then removed a prerolled joint. He lit it. "Been all over the news, mon." Curtis chuckled to himself. "I remember when that poor bastard was caught bangin' the babysitter."

"Old habits die hard."

Curtis raised an eyebrow. "You know something I don't?"

"His wife came to see me today." Jimmy lit a cigarette, giving Curtis a moment to let it sink in.

"How did she seem?"

"Sad, but not someone who just lost her husband sad."

Curtis took a pull from his joint. "A marriage of convenience. There's no way she would have put up with all his shit over the years and not get nothin' out of it. What she want?"

Jimmy recalled the other night. "I drove a girl over to the island, said she was his daughter. Apparently, she wasn't. Someone hired to you know."

"Damn." Curtis got the innuendo. "I guess old habits do die hard."

Jimmy handed Curtis the blurry photo that Lisa Brenner gave him. "She asked me if I could find her."

"Playing detective, huh?"

"I guess so."

Curtis used the flashlight on his phone to see the picture. "Not much of a photo."

"I know it's grainy, but it's all I have to work with. And this." Jimmy reached into his pocket and pulled out the dove pendant necklace. "She was wearing a necklace that looked something like this."

"Never seen it." Curtis inspected the pendant. "How do you know she's local?"

"I don't. I was hoping you know someone who does? I'll give you two hundred bucks?"

"You know I don't deal in skin Jimmy, right? Why she want to find this girl anyway?"

"Thinks she has something to do with his death."

"What do you think?"

"I just want to make some money."

Curtis's eyes widened and he exhaled a big cloud of smoke and said, "I know a guy."

From the way spoke Jimmy knew it was about to get dangerous.

12

"Play it cool," Curtis said as Jimmy pulled up to an old rundown house. The two men had left Curtis's house twenty minutes earlier, twisting and turning, snaking along the gloomy, narrow hillside roads. The wealth of St. Thomas evaporated, replaced by profound island poverty few outsiders ever saw. The crumbling concrete foundation all that remained of half-built abandoned houses.

"They don't take too kindly to outsiders," Curtis said and turned off his moped. Jimmy followed.

Jimmy glanced at the five men silhouetted on the porch of the house. Each had a red solo cup in their hand and were covered in jewelry: gold bracelets, rings, necklaces catching the light inside.

"You sure I'm safe here?" Jimmy was nervous. He had been in the Virgin Islands for seven years, but there were still parts of the island off-limits to strangers.

"One love, brotha," Curtis said, tapping his chest with his fist. "Douglas is a businessman. But be glad you didn't come alone."

Jimmy followed Curtis towards the house.

"Who dis?" one of the men said. Intimidating, to say the least, the man resembled one big muscle. His piercing, bloodshot eyes didn't help to calm Jimmy's nerves. He meant business.

"Just a friend," Curtis grinned, trying to lighten the situation. He gave the man two massive joints and leaned in and embraced him. Jimmy couldn't tell if Curtis knew the men or if he was acting extra friendly.

"Is Douglas in?" Curtis's voice cracked.

Not a good sign, Jimmy thought.

The man scanned Curtis up and down then raised an eyebrow at Jimmy.

"He's cool, just a friend," Curtis added.

After a moment that felt like hours, the man finally said, "In dah back." He pointed in the direction of the house. His coat opened enough for the butt of a silver pistol to glint in the moonlight. With a piece like that, Jimmy knew they weren't just selling pot. These guys, whoever they are, were serious people into some real shit.

When Jimmy and Curtis entered the house, they stepped through a vast cloud of smoke. Music blasted, the bass practically rattling the drinks off the table. Jimmy could barely think. Men dressed in all black lounged on couches, next to women in lingerie. Were they strippers, hookers? Jimmy couldn't tell, but he would have certainly put money on it.

In contrast to the strapped men wearing a thousand dollars' worth of jewelry outside, it didn't seem like anyone in the house noticed they were even there. They all seemed numb, in a drug-induced haze. Mesmerized by an O ring a woman exhaled as she slowly moved to the music.

"I bet they don't even know what game is on," Curtis said and nodded to the football game coming from the TV in the back of the room.

Jimmy and Curtis advanced into the kitchen, which quieted the music some. Dirty dishes stacked a foot high in the sink, while half-empty pizza boxes scattered the counter. Jimmy had examined filthy homes like this in the past, usually after a double murder or drug deal gone bad. Not the place he ever wanted to visit again.

Plastic beads blocked the next room's door frame, like some '70s horror or porno movie. Curtis glanced at Jimmy as if to say *You ready for this?*

Jimmy nodded. He didn't know why Curtis bothered to help him. He seemed just as nervous as him. Curtis moved the beads out of the way, and the two men went through.

Dimly lit, Jimmy squinted as they entered the dark room.

A massive man sat on a red velvet couch, a large joint dangling from his lips. He wore a black shirt, black glasses, and a huge gold chain. A woman on each arm naked, except for the thin piece of jewelry wrapped around her torso tickling the top of her pubic hair.

The man resembled an ancient king before gluttony was a sin. Jimmy knew this had to be Douglas.

Next to Douglas and his women, standing on the velvet couch's edges, two men wore black berets. A silver Glock pistol hung under their armpit.

"Curtis, why you botherin' me? Can't you see I'm busy?" Douglas announced. His voice was deep and breathy, like someone who hadn't exercised in years. Jimmy wondered if he could even perform for the girls on his arms or if this was the closest he got to intimacy.

Jimmy felt Curtis tense up.

Maybe this was a bad idea after all.

Suddenly Douglas burst into laughter and said, "You still fuckin' skinny." The tension in the room instantly went away. The women chuckled, and the two serious-looking men cracked a grin.

"You're wastin' your time with dah rasta vegan thing, mon." Douglas tipped his sunglasses to the tip of his nose and nodded to Jimmy, "Who dis?"

Jimmy's heart raced at the thought of being called out. Douglas and his militia bodyguards might be cool with Curtis, but that didn't mean they were okay with him.

"He's my friend, Jimbo," Curtis replied. "Down in Red Hook. My guy with the tourists—the boatman. He moves some stuff for us."

"Boatman?" Douglas said.

"Yea, he takes them out divin', you know, for fish?"

"Well, boatman," Douglas turned to Jimmy, "I guess I should be askin' you the questions. Why you come botherin' me? When you got a fine piece of pussy on each arm, do you want some stranger comin' and askin' favors?"

"No, no," Jimmy stuttered. "I didn't mean to bother you. I'm sorry."

"Well, you did bother me. Now, what you want?"

"I'm looking for a girl," Jimmy's said.

Douglas burst into laughter, then glanced at Curtis, "Is he for real? That's the dumbest fuckin' question I've ever heard. Take your pick, boatman. We got all sorts of girls here."

"I'm sorry, that's not what I mean." Jimmy felt like an idiot. He pulled out the blurry photo of Monica and showed it to Douglas. "You see her before? Curtis said you might be able to help me find her. She wore a necklace like this." Jimmy showed him the dove pendant.

Douglas leaned back and inspected the photo and necklace.

"That photo sucks, boatman, it's all blurry and shit." Douglas lifted the necklace into the light. "This is like a piece of trash you get down in Charlotte Amalie. I got nothing, mon."

"She was last seen on Little Saint George. Does that help?" Jimmy blurted out in desperation.

That appeared to get Douglas's attention.

"Little Saint George? You mean Fuck Island?"

"What?" Jimmy didn't understand.

Douglas put a new joint to his lips, and one of the girls lit it. "You livin' in a dream world, Jimbo," Douglas exhaled, "askin' me questions about that place. They wouldn't let me or any of my girls get a hundred feet near that spot. Probably let my fat ass drown in the water on the way."

"But have you seen her?" Jimmy asked.

"Nah, bro," Douglas leaned back against the couch. "Whatever you can imagine, times that by a thousand, because this shit is unbelievable. Check out the Free Love House in Charlotte Amalie. I bet they can answer some questions."

Jimmy had never heard of it. "The Free Love House? Where in Charlotte Amalie?"

"I don't know, bro," Douglas said. Jimmy could tell Douglas was becoming agitated by their presence. "I like this side of the island. It's quiet. I do my thing. No one bothers me."

Douglas shifted his attention back to Curtis. "Yo skinny, you better have brought your special recipe."

Curtis handed Douglas a paper bag, and Douglas removed a marijuana bud from inside. The crystals glistened in the golden room light.

"Still the best chef in town. Michelin certified—grade A shit." Douglas smiled and waved them good-bye. The two bodyguards crossed their arms. Their smiles were replaced by a stern 'don't fuck with me' look.

Jimmy knew it was time to go.

Ten minutes later, Jimmy and Curtis were back outside by their mopeds. Jimmy handed Curtis two hundred dollars. "I didn't know it was going to be like that. It's worth triple what I'm paying you."

"No worries, Jimbo. Sorry I couldn't help you more. You should ask the people workin' the ferries in Red Hook. They might have seen her."

"What about this Free Love House he mentioned? You heard of it?"

"Nah, mon." Curtis shrugged, then threw his leg over his moped. "Can you find your way back home?"

"No worries, brotha," Jimmy said.

Curtis disappeared down the dark road.

On the ride home, Jimmy thought about what he would tell Lisa Brenner the next time he saw her. Freedom Love House? Jimmy knew a lot of spots in Charlotte Amalie, but not that place. Jimmy was exhausted. It had been a long night, and nothing made sense. Everything seemed to be a dead end.

An hour later, when Jimmy finally returned to the dive shop parking lot, it wasn't the radiant full moon over the tranquil calm waters of the Pillsbury Sound that captured his attention, but the hazy dim glow of Little Saint George and all the questions it begged.

Perhaps it was the island that was the most intriguing mystery of all.

13

The next day it was back to the grind. Jimmy woke up with a hangover and took a group of divers out to the reef. They were real divers this time. No one asked for drugs or where the best place to get laid was. They actually wanted to know about the coral and different species of fish that lived in the area. Jimmy was professional as usual when he was with clients, and felt relieved to have diving take his mind off of Monica.

It wasn't until after the group of divers had finished for the day and Jimmy was cleaning their gear when he noticed a copy of *The New York Times* Joni had left behind.

The front page read: *US Senator and Former Presidential Hopeful Drowns in the Virgin Islands—Alcohol a Factor?*

Jimmy flipped the page. *The Future of the Internet Freedom Act?* was the headline of page two.

The noise of car tires crunching down the narrow island path drew Jimmy's attention from the newspaper article. A freshly polished black Mercedes with tinted windows entered the premises. Jimmy wasn't expecting anyone, and the thought of Joni stepping out of the car was comical.

The back window went down.

"Mr. Walsh," Lisa Brenner leaned into view, "Are you free?"

Jimmy was caught off guard, but then again, there were a lot of surprises lately.

"Call me Jimmy, please."

"How about James? Jimmy is so...well, it's just not as good, James."

Jimmy hadn't heard anyone call him "James" in years. Hayley was the last. It felt good he didn't realize how much he missed it.

"James is fine."

Lisa Brenner beamed. "Let's go for a ride."

The rest of Jimmy's day was free, but he still wanted to appear professional. After all, she was paying him a lot of money.

"Mrs. Brenner," Jimmy cautioned, "should I be seen with you in public? People might get the wrong idea."

"Call me Lisa," she said and lit a cigarette. "I don't care what people think, James. After years in the public eye, you learn to develop a thick skin."

"Well, Lisa, that's a lie," Jimmy raised an eyebrow. "Or else you would have gone to the police instead of me."

Lisa smirked. "A figure of speech. I suppose we all have our limits. Get in."

Jimmy got in the car.

Twenty minutes later, they were inside the security gate of a gorgeous home. Ferns and vegetation shrouded the estate from the street. Even with a steel gate, no one would have guessed what kind of house existed just seconds off the road. Massive granite columns reminiscent of ancient Greece stood erect at the front entrance. The residence was the most extravagant single-person home Jimmy had seen on St. Thomas.

Jimmy followed Lisa into the house.

Expensive artwork decorated the house. It all seemed like squiggles and shapes to Jimmy, but he was smart enough to know that if a rich person has this sort of art, it was expensive. Nevertheless, Jimmy wasn't impressed with what hung on the wall; he was more taken by the view.

Past the kitchen and the living room was a large window overlooking the Pillsbury Sound. St. John and Little Saint George were both visible as distant specks in the ocean.

"I always wondered what view the people who lived in these houses had," Jimmy said, still fascinated with the vista.

Lisa was clearly pleased with his reaction. She opened a bottle of gin and said, "Drink?"

"Sure." Jimmy never said no to a drink, and gazed at the blue water calmly caressing the shore.

"What do you like? We have everything."

"I'm kind of an 'all of the above' type of person. Whatever you're having is fine with me."

"I like that. Easy." Lisa poured two glasses.

A photo on the stainless steel end table next to the sofa drew Jimmy's attention. It was of Lisa, William Brenner, and another man. They all appeared happy. William had his arm around Lisa, and the three of them had a glass of champagne in their hands. The picture appeared like it was taken in St. Thomas. Lisa looked younger, but not by much. Maybe five or six years ago.

"Is this your place?" Jimmy asked Lisa as she finished mixing the drinks.

"No," she cleaned up the olive juice that spilled from the martinis. "It belongs to Jonathan Alderman."

"Who?" Jimmy asked. The name wasn't familiar to him.

Lisa strolled toward him. The summer dress showed off her figure. Her skin soft and clear, her breasts perfect for her petite frame. Her pedicured bare feet glided across the floor. "I thought everyone knew who he is." She paused and took a sip, moving the straw with her tongue ever so slightly. "He owns Little Saint George." She said it like it was common knowledge. "Sometimes we stay here, and sometimes we stay on the island."

Lisa handed Jimmy his cocktail.

"Is that Alderman in the photo?" Jimmy nodded at the picture.

"Yes."

"You look close. You friends?"

Lisa seemed to ignore the question.

"It's an old photo," she replied. "You like the drink?"

"Never met one that I didn't." Jimmy took a sip. "Forgive me for asking, but how long do you plan on staying here?"

Lisa twirled her hair. Was she coming on to him, he thought? If she wasn't, then she was indeed a heartbreaker in her day.

"I don't know how long I'll stay. I'm not sure if I'm up to leaving yet. It's so cold back home. Isn't that why you've stayed here all these years?"

Jimmy didn't remember telling her he was from a cold climate. But maybe it was a figure of speech. Everywhere is colder than here.

"The climate? Yes. I hate the cold."

"You must think I'm strange." Lisa took another sip.

"Why's that?"

Lisa moved closer. He was certain now; she was coming on to him.

"Here I am," she blushed. "Just lost my husband, and I'm talking about the weather."

"Every marriage is different."

"Were you married?"

Jimmy thought about Hayley and the moments they shared.

"No, but I came close to it."

Jimmy felt Lisa brush the side of his hand. "Well, I was married, but it wasn't real. It wasn't love. We both had our separate lives, you know?"

Jimmy considered leaving. He could go right now. Ask the driver to take him home. But something kept him there. She was beautiful. It had been so long since he had been with a woman.

Lisa brushed the front of his pants.

He closed his eyes.

His heart raced. He was nervous. Was this real?

Jimmy leaned over and kissed her. It was soft at first. Gentle. Then passionate. She grabbed him and pulled him closer. He could feel her nipples through her dress.

He rubbed against her and undid her backstrap; her dress dropped to the floor. She was stunning—her body in perfect condition, like an athlete twenty years younger. A small faded red heart tattooed just below her panty line hinted at a wild side in her youth.

Jimmy ran his hands down her back and over her thigh. He slipped her panties down to the ground. Her scent was intoxicating.

Jimmy picked Lisa up and carried her into the bedroom.

14

The following morning Jimmy was off from work, and he found himself at Marooned. The Senator wasn't even dead a week, and he had already slept with his wife. Jimmy had trouble wrapping his head around that one. Was he to blame or her?

"Drink?" Kate said. A damp towel over her shoulder from wiping down the bar.

Jimmy nodded but didn't make eye contact. Even though he hadn't dated Kate in almost a year, he still felt guilty for some reason. She even had been with the 'rich tourist' Eddie told him about, so why should he feel bad? Jimmy knew he still had feelings for her.

"What's wrong?" Kate smiled and put a cold Red Stripe in front of him. "Breakfast of champions. Cheer up. If you're worried you said something stupid the other night, don't stress. It wasn't anything I haven't heard you say before."

Kate laughed, and Jimmy grinned. Her smile was infectious. If she only knew what was running through his mind. He had slept with the woman who hired him to find out how her husband died.

"A long couple of days," Jimmy said, and almost drank the whole beer in one gulp.

"A bar is the closest thing to a confessional these days."

Jimmy glanced up from his drink. He always loved how she cheered him up when he was down.

"Nothing stays a secret in a bar."

Kate leaned in. "Try me?" Kate clasped Jimmy's hand. It had been so long since he had felt her touch him. He missed her; he missed what they had. "You know it was great seeing you the other night," she added.

Jimmy's heart skipped a beat. He wished she hadn't said that. Regret paralyzed his thoughts. Sleeping with Lisa Brenner was a mistake. He wished he could take it back. Jimmy took a deep breath and finished the beer.

"By any chance, have you heard of the Free Love House?"

"Free Love House?" Kate chuckled. "What's that? Sounds like a hippie commune."

Jimmy peeled the label off his empty beer bottle. "Yea, probably nothing." Jimmy pulled out the grainy photo of Monica Lisa had given him. "You wouldn't have seen this girl around, have you?"

Kate shook her head.

"She wore a necklace like this." Jimmy put the dove pendant necklace on the bar.

Kate didn't know.

"Okay, now I have to ask," Kate said, tossing the bar rag over her shoulder. "You playing detective now? What's this about?"

Jimmy adjusted himself on the bar seat. "Remember that girl I told you about? The one I drove to Little Saint George?"

Kate's eyes widened. "The Senator's daughter. Brenner, the one who drowned the other day."

Jimmy cracked his knuckles. "It seems she wasn't his daughter."

"Really?" Kate raised an eyebrow. "What does that mean?"

"That's what I'm trying to find out."

"Someone paying you?"

Jimmy was reluctant to say who. Perhaps it was the guilt. He dreaded Kate would somehow know he slept with Lisa just by speaking her name.

"His widow," Jimmy said quickly, lighting a cigarette.

Kate leaned over the bar and took another glimpse at the photo.

"She looks about Eddie's age. You should ask him. He's over at the dock."

Jimmy grinned. The thought of asking Eddie had never crossed his mind. If Monica was local to the island, then Eddie could help. Eddie was cool and handsome, popular with kids his age.

"Thanks," Jimmy said. He was glad he told Kate. He felt better, like there was still a connection between them. Perhaps their relationship wasn't dead after all.

He grabbed a fresh beer and walked toward the dock.

Eddie relaxed in his plastic beach chair at the end of the splintery pier waiting for boaters to pull in. He wore shorts, flip-flops, and a work t-shirt that said "Marooned" on the front. A cartoon of a drunken pirate passed out on an island was the bar logo. Jimmy always loved that image. He had a few of those shirts of his own from trivia night a while back.

"Hey, Eddie," Jimmy said, "I was hoping you could help me out with something?"

Eddie peered up from his phone. "Sure, what do you need?"

Jimmy gave him the photo of Monica.

"Have you seen this girl? She seems to be about your age. Called herself Monica."

Eddie squinted. "I don't know, Jimmy. I can barely make out her face. Sorry."

Jimmy reached into his pocket for the chain. The dove pendant glinted in the sun. "She wore a necklace like this."

"Where did you get that?" Eddie responded.

It was the speed at which Eddie answered that caught Jimmy's attention.

"I found it diving off Little Saint George." Jimmy trolled for more information. "You seen this before?"

Ed turned back to his phone. "Nope. Never."

"You sure?"

"Yea, Jimmy. I'm sure." Eddie seemed annoyed now.

Jimmy had questioned enough people to recognize when someone wasn't telling him the complete story. "Okay," Jimmy said, playing it cool. If Eddie did know something, he didn't want to spook him. "If you hear anything, let me know."

Jimmy shuffled back towards the bar. It wasn't the photo Eddie had responded to but the necklace—it seemed like he had seen it before, or seen one like it. Jimmy knew to play his hand close, gather more information. These types of riddles are a house of cards; they usually all fall at once.

Twenty minutes later, Jimmy was in downtown Red Hook doing more detective work. He felt better and a little like a cop again. His conversation with Eddie had given him some wind in his sails. He was onto something. Maybe the pendant meant something.

Dusk made everyone move even slower than they already did on St. Thomas. Tourists stumbled in and out of Red Hook shops with enormous grins on their faces, buying t-shirts and knick-knacks to bring home. Nobody was sober, and no one was too drunk. Everyone seemed to have a healthy buzz.

Jimmy parked his Vespa on the side of the street and walked to the ferry terminal. The terminal wasn't anything fancy: a concrete building with flaking yellow paint on the side. Next to the terminal, Jimmy ordered a daiquiri from a small tiki bar to pass the time as he waited for the next ferry to come in. When the ship finally arrived from St. Croix, he didn't recognize any faces.

Jimmy asked the dockworkers and ticket sellers if they had seen the girl in his photo or recognized the dove necklace.

Nothing.

Maybe this was the end of the line for today? Jimmy had searched everywhere in Red Hook and questioned everyone who might have seen her. It was getting late, and it was time to pack it up and stop playing private eye.

Jimmy threw his leg over his moped to head home, and suddenly a photo on the ferry bulletin board caught his eye. He got off his Vespa and moved closer to the board. Flyers of different bars, ferry time schedules, and live music scattered the board. Nestled in the mess of papers and information was a photograph. It wasn't a picture of Monica. It was of another girl, and she wore the dove pendant necklace. The girl seemed about the same age as Monica, young and beautiful, with her whole life ahead of her.

In black letters above the photograph, it read: Anna Gonzalez MISSING.

15

Jimmy ripped the photo off the bulletin board and took off on his moped.

"Welcome back," Kate said to Jimmy when he returned to the bar.

Jimmy lit a cigarette and took the beer Kate slid his way. It was dark now, and a lot of the regulars had slithered into Marooned since the morning.

"You know," Kate said, leaning in and whispering so others in the bar couldn't hear. "There was some woman in here just after you left asking about you." From the way Kate asked, Jimmy knew she wanted to know details.

"Really?" Jimmy slowly lifted the beer to his lips. Could Lisa Brenner be checking in on him? Why would she do that?

"What she look like?" Jimmy asked. The sensation of guilt sinking in. It had to have been Lisa. The last thing he wanted was for Lisa and Kate to ever meet,

and God help him if Kate ever found out they slept together.

"She wasn't ugly," Kate said, then leaned against
the bar.

Jimmy knew that was code for "she was jealous."
Kate took a swig of beer and wiped her lips with the
back of her hand. "A real bitch though. A pole stuck so
far up her ass she could barely sit down."

"What did she want?"

Kate shrugged. Jimmy knew Kate was playing him
a little bit. She had the information he wanted, and
she wasn't going to give it up easily.

"She wanted to know how often you came in, who
your friends were, that type of thing."

"And?" Jimmy said. He knew she wasn't telling
him everything.

"She did want to know what you did before coming
to the islands."

"What did you tell her?

"Nothing really, and I wasn't lying. You're a mystery to me, Jim. Just when I think I'm getting to know
you, you run away and put your head in the sand—or a
drink. You never did tell me everything that happened
in Boston."

That was true. Jimmy left that life behind when he
came here.

"And I never asked you about the rich tourist you
were seeing. It seems we both want to leave the past
where it is."

Kate smirked. "I would have told you. You just never asked."

"I don't want to know. I'm giving you your privacy."

"And I'm giving you yours. That's why I never asked you who the woman was."

"Maybe I should leave," Jimmy said. This conversation was getting a little too deep for his liking.

Jimmy paid.

Kate laughed. "What did I say, Jimmy—just when things are getting deep, you run off to put your head in the sand. See you in a month, right?"

Jimmy marched toward his moped.

"And one more thing," Kate said, walking out from behind the bar into the dirt parking lot. "I remember where I saw that necklace you found. I remember seeing Eddie talking to a girl wearing one."

Jimmy knew Eddie wasn't telling him the truth.

"Is he at the dock?" Jimmy was prepared to stroll down at the dock and stuff the picture of Anna Gonzalez in his face until he gave him answers.

"He left just before you got here. Probably at the Crab Shack."

Moments later, the Vespa tires shot up parking lot gravel as Jimmy raced back toward downtown Red Hook.

Club music from the Crab Shack could be heard all the way from the boat graveyard. Red Hook was in full party mode by the time Jimmy returned. Tourists stumbled around the streets with drinks in their hands while flashing dance lights bounced out of the different clubs.

Located in a strip mall parking lot near the ferry terminal, the Crab Shack was the place to be. Tables filled with young people surrounded the shack, which consisted of a bar and a dance floor.

During the day, the Crab Shack was a quaint restaurant where tourists ate seafood and had a cold drink, but at night, it turned into a night club. Unlike clubs and bars in Charlotte Amalie, the Crab Shack brought in both tourists and locals looking to have a good time.

A fog machine blasted Jimmy as he pulled his Vespa next to the club. Lasers and disco ball stars bolted across his face, moving with the beat of the music. Jimmy scanned the audience. People danced and then migrated to the tables scattered in the parking lot to talk and drink. The girls dressed their best, up on the latest trends and fashions, and the boys tried their hardest to get laid.

Jimmy spotted Eddie sitting with a group of girls. They seemed like tourists. Fresh tans, maybe sixteen or seventeen. Probably on vacation with their parents and getting their first taste of independence. Eighteen is the legal drinking age in the Virgin Islands, but the cops don't really care.

Jimmy nodded at Eddie and mouthed the words *Can I talk to you?*

Eddie didn't look too pleased that Jimmy had crashed his party. However, Jimmy wasn't going to leave until they spoke. Eddie seemed to get the point and walked toward Jimmy.

"What's up?" Eddie asked as the two found a place at the edge of the parking lot where they could hear each other.

Jimmy stared directly into Eddie's eyes and said, "Why did you lie to me about the necklace?"

"Come on, man," Eddie said, turning away.

Jimmy grabbed Eddie's arm. "This is serious."

"They have necklaces like that all over St. Thomas."

"They do?" Jimmy furrowed his brow. "Because I've never seen any before."

Jimmy showed Eddie the missing person's photo of Anna Gonzalez and pointed to the dove pendant around her neck.

"You know this girl?"

"Yes, I knew her, alright?" Eddie snapped. He ran his fingers through his hair and lit a cigarette. His hands were shaking. He was nervous, scared. "Where did you find the necklace?"

"I told you. I found it diving near Little Saint George." Jimmy showed Eddie the blurry photo of Monica again. "You know this girl too, right? I know you do. Don't lie to me."

"Man, you're in way over your head. This is deeper than you know." Eddie held up his hands and backed away. "Just stop. I can't be seen with you."

"Where is she?" Jimmy knew Eddie had more information.

"Let it go, man." Eddie walked backward toward the club.

"Are these girls connected?" Jimmy shouted over the sound of the music. "Have you heard of the Free Love House?"

"I'm done," Eddie shouted and disappeared into the crowd of people dancing in the fog.

Jimmy knew it was all connected somehow. It had to be: the missing girls, the dove pendant, the Free Love House, and the Island.

Jimmy was exhausted. He needed a break from all this. Let all the clues sink in. He needed sleep, some time to think.

A nightcap in his beach chair at the Dive Shop sounded like bliss. He would pick this all up in the morning.

Moments later Jimmy started up his moped and pulled out of the Crab Shack parking lot. Leaving all the young partiers and loud noises behind him. Jimmy hated those types of places. It was the only time he ever felt old. Watching young kids throwback without a care in the world, with so much of their life ahead of them, made him truly feel how much of his he had wasted.

Without Jimmy knowing, a black Escalade turned on its headlights and followed him down the road.

16

Jimmy glanced in his rearview mirror. The blue glow of halogen headlights caught his eye. Was he being trailed?

He accelerated the moped and quickly turned off the main road to see if the car continued to follow him. The headlights maintained their path, winding down the same dark and narrow road as Jimmy.

This didn't make any sense. Had someone been watching him? Maybe the woman who checked up on him at Marooned wasn't Lisa Brenner.

But who?

The dirt road leading to the Dive Shop was just up ahead. Jimmy pulled over to the side of the road to see if the car would stop. The black SUV buzzed by, barely missing him. Jimmy squinted, attempting to get a look in the window, but the car was too fast for him to make out anyone inside.

Don't be paranoid, Jimmy said to himself. *It was nothing. Nobody is following you. Your mind is just playing tricks on you.*

Five minutes later, Jimmy pulled into the Dive Shop driveway. Moonlight spilled in through the ferns above, lighting a patch of dirt where he parked the Vespa.

A car door slammed behind Jimmy and cut the night silence like a gunshot. Jimmy's head snapped in the direction of the noise.

Lisa Brenner walked out of the dark. Behind her was the black car Lisa had picked Jimmy up in before.

"Don't worry, I'm alone," she said.

"You have to stop sneaking up on me like that."

Lisa wore a long linen dress. The wind gently caressed the fabric, revealing the outline of her body. Her gold earrings caught the glint of moonlight reflecting off the water.

It was obvious she had been waiting for him, but for how long?

"Have you been checking up on me?" Jimmy asked, a little annoyed.

Lisa shrugged. "Just protecting my investment."

"I thought we wanted to keep this private?"

"I didn't tell her about us, if that's what you meant. You know, just that we were old friends."

Jimmy was relieved. The less Kate knew, the better.

"I didn't know there was an 'us'?" Jimmy raised his tone at the end as if he were asking a question.

"Relax, Jimmy, don't get serious." Lisa lit a cigarette. "It doesn't have to be anything. You don't need to go run off and bury your head in the sand." Lisa chuckled.

Kate had apparently told Lisa more than she had let on.

"Kate's a nice girl," Lisa said. "Old habits die hard, huh? Too bad you let her go."

Jimmy wandered toward the small bar on the dive dock and poured a shot of tequila.

"Who was better in bed?" Lisa asked with confidence in her skill.

Jimmy had had enough. He was tired of Lisa's games, and pulled out the missing person's photo of Anna Gonzalez.

"You seen this girl?"

Lisa studied the photo. "No. Who is she?"

"I don't know." Jimmy downed the shot and cracked open a beer. "Somehow, she's related to the other girl—Monica. They both have the same dove pendant."

"What do you think it means?"

Jimmy added rum and fruit punch to a plastic cup, stirred in ice, and handed it to Lisa.

"I don't know. You tell me?" Jimmy pulled the pendant out of his pocket.

Lisa shook her head. "Never seen it before."

"I was afraid you were going to say that."

Lisa drew Jimmy close to her and kissed him on the lips.

He froze. His lips like stone; he didn't kiss her back. Suddenly he sensed her hand down by his belt.

He glimpsed down and saw her put a few hundred dollars in his pants' pocket.

"Good job, Mr. Detective," she said.

Her breath was sweet from the rum punch, but made stale from the cigarette. She glanced at the dirty bar and then at the scratched boat, floating back and forth at the dock.

"You know, James? You don't have to stay here. Stay with me." She licked her lips and smiled. "I'll even let you drive."

Jimmy backed away from Lisa. "Next time. I'm just not feeling well."

Lisa swallowed hard. Clearly annoyed, she walked back to the car. Lisa was definitely the type of woman that rarely felt rejected, and with good reason. She was the type of woman men fantasized about.

"Keep in touch, James." Lisa returned to the town car.

Jimmy was relieved when the vehicle disappeared down the narrow dark jungle road. He wanted to be alone, but instead was left with thoughts of the missing girls: Monica and Anna. Then he thought of the girl with the pink streak in her hair. She seemed so scared—they were all so young.

With a sudden flash of memory, he thought of Boston. The trial. And what had happened, the events that led him to the Virgin Islands. The screams of children still rang in his ears from the day that changed the rest of his life.

Jimmy Walsh poured another drink.

17

YEARS EARLIER.

"Officer James W. Balzano, can you tell me what happened on October 13th?" The lawyer was firm and sobering with her questioning.

Jimmy surveyed the courtroom. This was his final day on the stand, and the first time he'd glanced up and made eye contact. The faces of the widowed officers and the parents of murdered children glared back.

Hayley Diaz sat in the back of the courtroom near the door.

Tears swelled in Jimmy's eyes. His stomach churned. He wanted to vomit.

"I know this isn't easy, Officer Balzano," the lawyer continued. Her voice was soft and calm this time, like she was his friend, and they were all alone. *Just tell me your secrets, lay your whole heart and soul on the line for others to judge.*

Jimmy wanted to scream; he swallowed, a massive knot forming in his throat. The eyes of the court were on him, anticipating, judging his next move.

Jimmy wiped the sweat off his forehead with the back of his hand and seized the glass of water on the mahogany partition in front of him. The cold water soothed his dry throat.

When Jimmy spoke, nothing came out. He took a breath, readjusted his nylon courtroom chair. The events of that day were clear. As the *Globe* wrote, it was a "massacre."

Jimmy could still smell the scent of the freshly paved asphalt of the high school parking lot like it was yesterday. The screams and pop of gunfire woke him up at night.

How could he ever forget?

Jimmy Walsh began to speak:

"I was eating lunch in my patrol car when I got the call that there were shots fired at Tarboro High School. At first, I couldn't believe it. Not here. It couldn't be. Not in this town.

"By the time I got to the school—maybe five minutes later—I had feared the worst. Kids and teachers were already running out. They were yelling; it was a frenzy. I saw blood on one kid's shirt. I didn't know if it was his or someone else still inside."

"You were the first responder?" the lawyer asked.

Jimmy nodded.

"Did you go in right away?"

"There were kids everywhere."

"So you froze?" The lawyer's demeanor changed. She was out to get him now.

Jimmy licked his lips. "I didn't freeze."

"There were reports that you sat in your car for five minutes?"

Jimmy shook his head. "That's not true."

"Isn't your job to 'serve and protect'? People were dying. Kids, twelve-year-old kids."

Jimmy tried to swallow, but the knot in his throat stopped him.

"Were you scared, Mr. Balzano?" There was a glint in her eyes like she was proud of what she was doing to him. Destroying an honest cop trying to do his job

"Of course I was scared. No matter how much you train, you can never prepare yourself for when something like this happens for real."

The lawyer raised her eyebrow. "So you did freeze? You sat there?"

Jimmy peeked out at the courtroom from under his brow. Angry eyes radiated back.

"I was assessing the situation," Jimmy continued. "Looking for entrances, trying to see if the shooter was outside, among the kids, or still inside."

"Did you see the shooter?"

"I did. I could see him through the window."

"Did you see what type of weapon he had?"

"I did. He had a Glock."

"Only one weapon, no assault rifle?"

"That's right."

The lawyer turned toward the jury. "So with your training Officer Balzano, you might have prevented, maybe not all the deaths, but you could have saved the lives of young Sarah McHale, Danny Pertolli, Jeremy Cortez?"

The lawyer flashed 8x11 photographs of the slain children. Each photo was a child full of life, happily playing baseball, soccer, laughing with friends and family at Christmas or birthday parties. The lawyer presented another photo of a handsome young man.

"Mr. Ferris was the new history teacher. Two weeks on the job—Officer Balzano, you saw the shooter through the window. You knew what weapon he had."

Jimmy wanted to leave. He needed to get away from everything. Go and hide, never come back. He wanted to put on a mask so no one could ever see him again. He thought of the headlines calling him a: COWARD, Not a REAL Man, PART of The Problem.

"Officer Daniels, who gave his testimony yesterday, told us it was him and Officer Caroline Perry who found you still in your car—is that true?"

Jimmy nodded.

"Please speak into the microphone," the lawyer directed.

Jimmy pitched forward. "Yes."

"What happened next?"

"I followed Officer Daniels and Officer Perry toward the entrance of the school."

Jimmy rubbed the sweat from the top of his lip. His hand shook.

"And?" the lawyer pressed.

Jimmy glanced up. "That's when McLaughlin came out from around the corner," Jimmy bit his lip, "and shot Officer Caroline Perry and Officer Daniels."

"Killed Officer Perry." The lawyer brought up the official police photograph of Caroline Perry, young and beautiful with her full life ahead of her as a police officer.

Jimmy acknowledged, "Yes. Officer Perry was shot."

"Was it Officer Daniels who saved your life?" The lawyer pointed to Daniels, dressed in his police uniform, sitting in a wheelchair in the front of the court.

"Yes."

"You knew the layout of the school. You knew the shooter was going to be there. Did you ever think to tell either Officer Perry or Daniels that you had seen the shooter through the window and knew his weapon?"

Jimmy glanced in the back of the courtroom. He hoped to lock eyes with Hayley. He needed her support, her wisdom, her love, but she was gone.

Jimmy felt broken, abandoned. Alone. Exactly the same way he knew the parents of the children felt. He could have done more. He could have saved the children, Officer Perry.

James Walsh Balzano could no longer bear to look Officer Daniels or any of the parents in their eyes. He had to save himself. That was all he could do now, so he cleared his throat, leaned into the microphone, and lied, "I told Officer Perry where the shooter was."

The crowd gasped.

"Liar!" Officer Daniels yelled from his chair.

The attendees erupted in shouts. Parents screamed, officers yelled. Bailiffs moved to secure the courtroom as the judge slammed his gavel down.

"Order," the judge yelled, "I will not have chaos in my courtroom."

Jimmy leaned back in the grey vinyl chair. The truth would never come out. It was his word against Officer Daniels. Everyone else was dead.

Even if it crushed him to lie, he had to keep his dignity. For the first time in his life, Jimmy Walsh knew what it was like to be public enemy number one and completely alone.

18

Jimmy woke up with a jolt in a pile of empty beer cans and Doritos chips scattered across the dive boat. His heart raced. Sweat oozed from his pores. He felt like he was having a heart attack. His heart thumped, his breathing labored. Panic spread through his nervous system like electricity as he replayed the events of the school massacre.

He wished he could take it all back. Start over again, go back and get out of the police car and kill the shooter. He could have maybe saved ten lives. His thoughts turned to Monica and Anna Gonzalez. What happened to them? Tragedy seemed to follow him everywhere.

Jimmy took a deep breath. His heart slowed down; a sense of calm returned. Just a panic attack, he thought. Maybe a hangover, thin blood—all of the above. He wondered how much his lifestyle had taken its toll on his body. He knew days, years had been taken off his life from not only the stress but the drinking and smoking.

Jimmy never intended on sleeping on the dive boat indefinitely. When he first arrived on St. Thomas, he had an apartment in Charlotte Amalie, but after the year it took to get his Dive Master's license, the quieter side of the island called his name.

Red Hook was the perfect place, and Joni was the perfect boss—she didn't give a shit. She wanted her privacy and peace of mind like everyone else who comes to the Virgin Islands to start anew.

He gulped a bottle of water and let the boat calmly sway back and forth. Jimmy had had enough surprises the past few days, so a night on the water was refreshing. He washed his face and brushed his teeth with a few more bottles of spring water to freshen up. Even after brushing his teeth and a piece of gum, he could still taste the stale Doritos and old beer.

He lit a cigarette--that always helped--then hauled up the anchor and headed back to shore.

When he came into view of the Dive Shop dock from the water, Jimmy noticed cardboard boxes stacked on top of each other at the end of the pier.

Joni sat in Jimmy's beach chair wearing her massive sun hat while fanning herself.

"What's all this?" Jimmy yelled from the boat.

Joni's big frame struggled to get out of the low chair. "Some guy shows up in a car an hour ago and says he wants you to bring these boxes over to Little Saint George."

Jimmy parked the boat at the dock. Joni guided the edge of the vessel so it wouldn't rub against the wood.

"What's in em?" Jimmy asked.

Joni kicked one of the boxes; something shook inside. "I was hoping you would tell me."

"Beats me. You look?"

"They're taped shut."

"Why me? There must be a thousand other boats that ship stuff." Other than divers, Jimmy had never been asked to bring anything anywhere, especially not to Little Saint George. That seemed odd.

"All I know, Jimmy, is that he specifically asked for you."

Jimmy removed his pocket knife and opened a box.

"Wine glasses? Jimmy said. There had to be hundreds of them.

Joni scratched her head. "The guy said he would pay you when you drop the boxes off. He said you knew where the island landing was."

Jimmy remembered the dock where he had dropped Monica off that night. He wasn't opposed to making a few more bucks, and maybe he could find some more information on Monica.

"Can you help me load these up?" Jimmy said.

"Nope," Joni replied. "I just had to wait here a full hour for you to get your hungover ass back here. I did my part, now don't be afraid to give me a share of whatever those rich son-of-a-bitches pay you over there. And don't be cheap. I've heard the stories. I know they pay well."

Joni left in her Jeep Wrangler, and Jimmy spent the next forty minutes packing the boxes and securing the cargo to the boat.

Jimmy arrived at the Little Saint George pier an hour later. The small enclave on the southern part of the island looked different in the day. Without the pale moon above and the flaming tiki-torches, the mystique was gone, replaced by a simple wooden dock located at the private island's lush base.

Krauthammer and Ramirez greeted Jimmy with a scowl as he slowed the boat. The two men wore collared shirts, khaki shorts, and white boat shoes.

"You guys look adorable," Jimmy shouted from the boat as it glided into the dock. "I know a really classy bar in Red Hook you should check out."

Neither of the men were amused. Krauthammer crossed his arms and spat in the water. They were giving Jimmy the silent treatment, but he didn't care. Jimmy was about to toss the boat line to Ramirez, but noticed his left arm was in a sling.

"You slip in the shower?" Jimmy said.

Ramirez rolled his eyes. "Good thing I punch with my right."

Jimmy tossed the line to Krauthammer. He enjoyed pissing these pricks off. Somebody summoned him to the island for some other reason than hauling wine glasses. They could have paid anyone to carry that shit over. They wanted something from him. They needed him, and Jimmy liked that.

"Who pays me?" Jimmy said after unloading the boxes onto the dock.

"He wants to see you," Krauthammer mumbled.

"Who wants to see me?"

"Mr. Alderman."

Jimmy remembered the photo in Lisa Brenner's house, but ever the wise-ass, Jimmy couldn't resist. "Who is Mr. Alderman?"

"He owns the island, asshole," Ramirez chimed in.

"Oh yes, him. I didn't know that was a thing—owning an island."

Krauthammer offered his hand to help Jimmy out of the boat. Jimmy studied the massive hand that had punched him in the gut a few days ago. The hand was hairy and resembled a grizzly bear paw.

Jimmy cocked his head. "So you're sure I'm on the guestlist this time? I don't want to get punched in the gut again."

Krauthammer's melon-sized head nodded up and down. Jimmy realized Krauthammer wasn't like a bear anymore. He was an obedient pit-bull. Jimmy seized Krauthammer's hand and his arm was almost ripped out of the socket as Krauthammer pulled him from the boat to the dock.

"This way," Krauthammer bellowed.

Jimmy was nervous. Alderman may have called him to the island for a reason; instinct told him to keep his guard up. Powerful people all over the world have one thing in common: they want to keep their control and will do anything to protect it. Having someone like Krauthammer and Ramirez patrolling the palace gate and the Pillsbury Sound as a moat proved that this island was in every sense a castle. And castles have kings.

Ramirez waited behind while Jimmy followed Krauthammer up the narrow path into the island.

19

"Take it the conference is over?" Jimmy asked Krauthammer once they entered the amphitheater. The deserted theater looked different in the daytime. Smaller, less glamorous, but still impressive with its concrete structure and seating.

"Finished yesterday," Krauthammer replied. "But some of the guests have decided to stay a little longer."

"The death of the Senator didn't ruin anyone's vacation, huh?"

Krauthammer ignored Jimmy and lead him toward the exit, a flat limestone path on the other side of the concrete amphitheater. Jimmy remembered this exact spot. It was the last place he saw Monica and Senator Brenner alive. She was talking to the girl with the pink streak in her hair. They both appeared scared, like something bad was about to happen.

Jimmy and Krauthammer exited the amphitheater. Tropical birds and the scent of fresh flowers greeted Jimmy on the other side. It was easy to forget the brutalist architecture of the concrete theater. Quiet and peaceful, he felt like he was back in paradise—the garden of Eden. The green grass was perfectly manicured, and resembled a country club golf course. Massive palm trees sprouted up along the limestone walkway.

Twenty thatched-roof bungalows, which Jimmy assumed were luxury guest houses, were tucked away in the ferns and bushes on each side of the path. Privacy was paramount. The landscaping alone cost more than Jimmy's boat.

Housekeepers and waitresses carrying trays and linen bounced from bungalow to bungalow, tidying up after the guests and offering freshly squeezed pineapple juice. Each hostess was dressed in the island uniform: white shorts and a polo shirt with a palm tree emblem on the breast pocket.

The principal island compound lay at the end of the pathway like a grand southern plantation. The architecture was a mixture of white stucco plaster and Roman opulence with four massive columns at the entrance.

Jimmy accompanied Krauthammer around the villa, where a massive deck wrapped the compound. The view was gorgeous. It was the exact opposite view from the house that Lisa Brenner stayed in. The crystal clear blue water of the Pillsbury Sound in all its grandeur made Little Saint George truly feel like heaven.

A thumping sound and heavy breathing came from around the corner. A strange noise that Jimmy couldn't place. At Krauthammer's insistence, Jimmy approached the noise.

A shirtless man glistening in sweat threw punches and kicks at a trainer, who took each hit with padded gloves.

The man acknowledged Jimmy's presence, then threw a few final blows even more aggressively than the previous.

"Nice to finally meet you, Mr. Walsh," the man said. He breathed heavily as his trainer unwrapped his fists.

"Jimmy," he answered, trying his best to appear unimpressed by the man's physique or ability to fight.

"Right, Jimmy." The man smirked at Krauthammer like there was some inside joke between the two. "My name is Jonathan Alderman."

"Jonathan? Not John or Jay?"

Alderman wasn't impressed at Jimmy's sense of humor.

"Why did you want to see me?" Jimmy wanted to get right to the point.

Alderman grabbed a towel from his trainer and wiped the sweat from his face and chest, then gestured at Krauthammer and the trainer *that will be all*.

Both men left the deck and vanished into the massive estate, leaving Jimmy alone with Alderman.

"Jimmy, please sit," Alderman said with a newfound charm. He gestured at one of the steel deck chairs and smiled. "It's my job to know who comes on and off my island." Alderman put on a bathrobe and turned to admire the view. "It's beautiful, don't you think?"

Jimmy agreed. "This is paradise."

"That's exactly how I feel. It's my sanctuary. This is where I truly feel at home." Alderman sat opposite Jimmy and tapped a laptop on the coffee table. The screen turned on. "Even if I can't get away from work completely. Besides the unfortunate event with Senator Brenner, which I imagine you've heard of, I think this year's Cyber Talks was a success."

"Life goes on, huh?" Jimmy said sarcastically. He suspected this meeting had something to do with Brenner and the girl. He just didn't know in what way.

Alderman gazed at the sea as if pondering Jimmy's last statement. "Life does go on," Alderman repeated. "I knew you would understand." Alderman poured a wine glass of San Pellegrino sparkling water that had been chilling in a bowl of ice. "Are you a tech guy, Jimmy?"

Jimmy hoped Alderman would just get to the point and give him his money for hauling all that shit to the island, but he played nice and shrugged. "I use a navigation watch when I scuba dive."

"Of course," Alderman seemed delighted, "technology is everywhere, and with that, so is social media." Alderman took a sip of water and let out an over-exaggerated exhale, then proceeded, "With Cyber Talks, I'm striving to bring together the world's most illustrious and influential people to help foster and bring a climate of understanding and civility to the internet."

Jimmy couldn't help himself. Keeping his mouth shut when assholes were spewing bullshit was never a specialty of his, even if he did want the money. Jimmy lit a cigarette. "So a bunch of rich people trying to decide how the peasants should live? Where can I sign up?"

Alderman leaned back in his chair. "I take it you don't appreciate my philanthropy?"

"It's better than hoarding money. Spread the wealth, you know?" Jimmy ashed his cigarette into an empty wine glass. "Speaking of money?"

"Jimmy," Alderman said sternly. "I know a young girl came to see you the night of Senator Brenner's death. I was the one that supplied Mrs. Brenner with the photo—the one she gave to you."

Jimmy was relieved that Alderman was finally talking about why he was really here.

"You know I was Senator Brenner's largest contributor when he ran for President? I have a long history with the family. Unfortunately, the Senator wasn't as discrete in his personal life as he should have been. His wife has suffered dearly for it."

Jimmy thought about Lisa. That day at the house. Her face of ecstasy as he took her on the bed.

Alderman leaned forward. "I've noticed you've been spending a lot of time with her."

Jimmy swallowed. How much did he know?

"Even visiting my house on St. Thomas."

Jimmy thought of the night the black SUV followed him. Maybe it was Alderman keeping track of him.

Jimmy put out the cigarette, then tossed it in the wine glass and said, "I'm just helping a grieving widow."

"Of course." Alderman's mouth curved up, giving the faintest sign of a grin. "Are you sleeping with her? They did have an interesting marriage arrangement."

"Do you have an interest in other people's wives?"

Alderman leaned back. "Do you? Be careful with her. She's not as innocent as she seems."

Jimmy stood up. That very fact had crossed his mind before. "It's been nice talking to you." Jimmy turned to leave, and then paused. "Out of curiosity, how do you think that girl Monica ended up on the guest list?"

"Who knows? It's public knowledge that William Brenner was unable to control his appetite. I learned that the hard way during the Presidential primaries, and it cost me millions."

"I see. And why did you have me bring over all those boxes of wine glasses?"

"I figured you could use the cash."

"Is that it?"

"I'm a businessman," Alderman said, standing up and adjusting his bathrobe. "How do you think it looks when a US Senator drowns on my island—and then someone like you is running around town asking if they knew a girl, who happens to be the last girl who slept with him?"

Gone were the charm and pleasantries of Alderman's easy demeanor. "It looks bad, Jimmy. I run an international conference here, so I can't have journalists or private detectives snooping around. I will talk with Mrs. Brenner and make sure you are well compensated for bringing over the shipment of wine glasses."

"How well compensated?"

"Three thousand," Alderman said.

Jimmy was speechless. He couldn't believe it.

Before Jimmy could shout "yes," Alderman said, "Fine, five thousand. Krauthammer will see that you are taken care of. I trust this investigation is over?"

"Done," Jimmy responded.

Five thousand dollars, cash. That was the most Jimmy had gotten for doing nothing in a long time.

"Goodbye, Mr. Walsh. Or should I say, Balzano?"

Jimmy froze. He had never told anyone on St. Thomas his real last name, not even Kate or Joni.

Alderman grinned. "I told you I like to know who comes on my island. Have a nice day."

Alderman disappeared into his villa.

20

Krauthammer handed Jimmy an envelope with five thousand dollars in it. He didn't even bother to count it, plus someone with that kind of money tended to round up instead of down. It was heavier than he expected. Jimmy felt like he had won the lottery.

A part of Jimmy wanted to ask how Alderman obtained his real name, but then thought against it. People like Alderman had connections and channels to acquire information in ways Jimmy couldn't think of.

Just take the money and run, he thought.

Krauthammer ushered Jimmy off the deck and away from Alderman's villa. Jimmy insisted on taking a detour to the thatched-roof bar next to the first bungalow. Rum punch had been a staple in the Caribbean since the first pirate fell off a boat. Jimmy wasn't going to waste his opportunity to try the rum punch of Little Saint George.

Jimmy drank two rum punches and had another cigarette before Krauthammer grabbed him by the arm and said, "Let's go."

Jimmy didn't mind. He had a nice buzz, a pocket full of money, and no cares in the world. It was dusk, and the sun was sweet, like a massive orange lollypop melting at the horizon. He looked forward to the joint he was going to smoke on the boat ride back.

Jimmy was just about to enter the amphitheater when he suddenly bumped into a hostess coming in the opposite direction. He spilled his drink and caused the woman to drop the stack of white linen sheets she was carrying.

"Sorry." Jimmy felt bad. It was his fault; he wasn't paying attention. He quickly dropped to the ground and started to pick up the bedsheets that had scattered in the wind.

"Sorry, sir," the girl quickly said, falling on the ground to catch the sheets.

"It was my fault." Jimmy handed her the sheets he had collected and noticed it was the girl with the pink streak in her hair. The girl he had seen with Monica that night before Krauthammer had dragged him out.

"No, sir. I'll do it." The girl's voice cracked as she spoke.

Jimmy sensed fear and noticed the girl was looking up at Krauthammer, who glared back at her.

She was terrified of him.

"Let's go, Jimmy," Krauthammer ordered. "She'll clean it up."

A glint of silver around her neck caught Jimmy's eye. He couldn't believe it. She was wearing the same dove pendant necklace that Monica and Anna Gonzalez wore. The same one that he discovered not far off the shore of this island.

Krauthammer paced ten feet away. Jimmy could tell he was annoyed.

Jimmy wanted to speak to the girl, but he knew she wouldn't talk if she was afraid, especially if Krauthammer was there.

Jimmy locked eyes with her. He knew she remembered him. Monica must have told him that was how she'd gotten to the island.

Jimmy moved to block Krauthammer's sight of her and continued to pick up towels.

Jimmy whispered, "Your necklace, where did you get it?"

The girl peered up at Krauthammer to discern if he was watching. He was on his phone.

"The Freedom Dove House," the girl whispered back.

The Freedom Dove House? Jimmy said to himself.

"Where's Monica?" Jimmy whispered.

"I can't talk to you."

"Anna Gonzalez?"

No response.

"Please, I want to help," Jimmy pleaded. He could tell she was terrified.

"Let's go, Jimmy," Krauthammer yelled. "I said she would do it!"

"Where's the Freedom Dove House?" Jimmy whispered.

The girl with the pink streak in her hair finished picking up the last of the towels. "Charlotte Amalie," she muttered before taking off in the direction of the bungalows.

Freedom Dove House, Jimmy said to himself again. Then it clicked in his mind; The *Freedom Dove House* was the *Free Love House*. They were the same thing—just a play on words. It never even crossed his mind.

Jimmy felt Krauthammer's large paw on his shoulder and understood. He had to go.

21

The next morning Jimmy cleaned himself up and prepared the forty-minute trip to Charlotte Amalie. He showered and shaved in the outdoor shower next to the Dive Shop. He ran a comb through his hair for the first time in weeks. He looked in the mirror. The booze hadn't taken every ounce of youth yet. He was still handsome. He put on his best clothes: khaki pants and a light blue button-up shirt and walked towards his Vespa.

His stomach twisted into a knot at the thought of the stack of one hundred dollar bills in his pocket. He felt guilty for accepting it. He should have asked more questions and not feared Krauthammer.

The girl with the pink streak in her hair had been frightened. He could have done more, at least something. He began to sense that same feeling from all those years ago, watching those kids scream and doing nothing. Gunshots rang in his ears, the scent of blood still fresh in his nose. He knew he got off easier than he should have. He got lucky; they didn't. They may have taken his badge and his reputation, but he stayed out of prison. He got a second shot at life, but why? He didn't deserve it.

Get ahold of yourself, he told himself. *It wasn't like you could have fought Krauthammer on the island and saved the girl. Escape on the boat into the sunset, like some fuckin' movie.*

Jimmy knew he had to play it slow, easy. Not make too many waves. Find the Freedom Dove House; that was his plan.

Fifteen minutes later, Jimmy entered downtown Red Hook. It was quiet. The tourists were probably sleeping off their hangovers. Just as Jimmy passed Marooned and the boat graveyard, a siren sounded from behind him. Jimmy glanced in his rearview mirror. Officer Ajax Cason large frame was plopped on top of a small black and white island police motorcycle. Jimmy had never scene Cason on bike duty before—something was off. Cason flashed his lights.

Jimmy pulled over and waited for Cason to approach.

"I thought you were a boat cop?" Jimmy joked, trying to keep the mood light.

"Not today," Cason was stern. More than usual. "Where you headed, Jimbo?" Cason moved closer. His massive leather biker boots crunching the loose gravel below.

"Charlotte Amalie."

Cason paused and furrowed his brow. With Jimmy still on his moped, Cason towered over him.

"I've been hearin' rumors about you, Jimbo," Cason said.

Strange, Jimmy thought. It seemed like Cason was interrogating him. Not overt, but his tone was different than other times they had met. Cason was serious and asking questions like a cop looking for something.

"What about?" Jimmy said calmly. St. Thomas was a small island, and word traveled fast. Jimmy was curious about what people were saying about him.

"You've been spendin' time with Mrs. Brenner?" Cason asked.

Jimmy hesitated. He didn't want to lie, but he didn't want anyone to know his business either.

"Small island." Cason crossed his arms. "It doesn't strike you as a little odd that the wife of Senator is hangin' round with you?"

Jimmy knew it was odd, but so what?

"Especially when her husband's death is still under investigation?"

Jimmy swallowed. "Under investigation? I thought you said he drowned?"

"Senator Brenner hit his head and THEN drowned. Sometimes it's the little details that make an investigation."

Jimmy tried to read between the lines. Did Cason suspect Mrs. Brenner? "You don't honestly think she had something to do with it?" he said.

Cason raised an eyebrow. "They didn't exactly have the best marriage. Be careful, Jimbo." Cason touched the brim of his helmet like a cowboy and said, "Have a good day in the big city. The weather's supposed to be perfect." He grinned and lowered his sunglasses. "Be careful out there. You never knew who's watching."

Jimmy watched Cason get on his motorcycle and ride away. Jimmy checked the mirror again to see if anyone else was watching. Sunlight cut through the jagged masts of the boat graveyard casting sharp shadows across the deteriorating island road. He was alone, but still couldn't shake the feeling that the whole island was somehow watching his every move.

22

With a population of 18, 481, Charlotte Amalie was a big city in the Virgin Islands. Anywhere else, it would have been a town, but a town with a deep-water harbor that over the years had brought everything from Danish colonists, to pirates, to slaves to the island. Now the port harbored massive cruise ships delivering millions of delighted tourists.

Jimmy relished coming to the big city now and then. The cruise ships alone were a sight. Carnival, Celebrity, Royal Caribbean Cruises Lines. Floating municipalities that towered over the capital, transporting the party and most importantly the economic lifeline from island to island.

In addition to the luxury cruise lines, private yachts peppered the crystal clear blue water, each searching for their utopia.

Jimmy buzzed through downtown Charlotte Amalie on his Vespa. Any other day he would have stopped and had a fresh piece of fish and a cold drink while he watched the visitors, but today he kept moving.

For the next two hours, Jimmy drove around the city, asking the locals if they have heard of the Freedom Dove House. Jimmy showed them the dove pendant to see if that helped jog their mind. Most had no clue what Jimmy was asking, and the few locals who did know told him of a place on the other side of the city. "The edge," they called it.

The outskirts of Charlotte Amalie resembled a ghost town. It wasn't a spot where tourists or even the locals visited. Half constructed buildings and abandoned business strewn across the overgrown land. Weeds crawled up the cement foundations and swallowed old cars. This was the sad part of the Caribbean, where paradise ended.

There was nothing out here, Jimmy thought.

Just when he was about to turn around, Jimmy saw something silver on top of a distant roof reflecting the sun.

Jimmy proceeded down the unpaved, long dusty road toward the building. Gone were the lush vegetation that provided shade from the oppressive tropical sun—dry straw grass and wandering tumbleweeds fluttering in the breeze.

"Welcome to the Freedom Dove House School for Girls," a tin sign read. The aluminum signed flapped in the wind, making the sound of thunder.

A silver dove sat on top of the school. The building was a simple two-story cement compound with flaking murals of women painted on the side. Girls aged twelve to sixteen played basketball on the two cracked courts next to the school.

Upon seeing Jimmy enter the school grounds, a slim woman, maybe mid-thirties, dressed in a long skirt and polo shirt, walked out from the school entrance.

"Are you lost, sir?" the woman asked. Her voice was pleasant and welcoming.

Jimmy drew the moped to a halt. "I don't think so."

"Can I help you?"

Jimmy glanced up at the silver dove on the roof of the school. "Is this the Freedom Dove House?"

"Yes. May I ask who you are?"

Jimmy could tell she was now growing suspicious. "Oh yes, I'm sorry." Jimmy swiftly rummaged for a story, and then it came to him. "I'm with...Mr. Alderman. I just started last week. He told me to come by and learn more about the program?"

The woman relaxed her shoulders as if relieved. "Of course," she smiled. "Please come in out of the sun. My name is Susie Walker. I'm the principal at the Dove School. How's Mr. Alderman doing?"

"Saving the world," Jimmy smirked, then followed her into the building.

Cabinets full of school trophies and team photographs throughout the years lined both sides of the school entrance. White Doves, the school mascot, were everywhere.

"I've never actually met Mr. Alderman myself. I hear he is very private." Ms. Walker was pleasant and accommodating. Jimmy felt terrible that he had to lie. She gestured at the school walls. "If it weren't for Mr. Alderman and his generosity, none of this would be here."

Jimmy pried for more information. "So, Mr. Alderman helps you out a lot, huh?"

"Of course. He completely funds us."

Jimmy glanced down at the giant dove, tiled into the floor. "I like the logo."

Ms. Walker beamed proudly, "Yes. It symbolizes hope. A better future. These girls have suffered enough."

Jimmy wanted to know more, but he couldn't be noticeable. He was supposed to know all of this already.

"Yes, I saw the dove on a necklace on a girl on Little Saint George."

Ms. Walker nodded. "Every rescued girl gets a dove necklace."

Jimmy noted her use of the word *rescued*.

Ms. Walker continued, "Little Saint George is our best program. Tourism and hospitality are the biggest industries on the Virgin Islands, but we also have work-study programs at hair salons and other local businesses. We would love all our girls to get into college, but unfortunately, the world doesn't work that way. We focus on practical life skills."

Jimmy responded as if he knew all this already. "Can you tell me a little bit more about the school—do the girls live here? Where are their parents?"

Ms. Walker seemed confused. "Mr. Alderman didn't tell you?"

Jimmy searched for a follow-up. He didn't want to blow his cover. Something. Anything.

"Oh, he did," Jimmy insisted. "But it's better to get it from someone like yourself, who's in the field doing a great job. Not us in our ivory tower."

"Of course," Ms. Walker smiled and took the compliment. "Freedom Dove House is a shelter. All our girls come from traumatic situations. We try to prepare them for society the best we can and then set them free at eighteen."

"Free doves."

"That's right. Most have been victims of sex trafficking, prostitution, assaults, abuse. A lot of the time, it's their families that trafficked them. The majority of the girls here aren't even from the Virgin Islands."

"Really?"

"Puerto Rico, Dominican Republic. Most of the time, the mothers are kids themselves."

Jimmy examined the trophies and school photos behind the glass cabinets. Ms. Walker appeared pleased that he showed interest.

"The girls play other islands in the Caribbean. We believe sports help give them confidence and build teamwork."

Jimmy agreed.

A photo behind the glass abruptly caught his eye. "Who's that?"

Ms. Walker leaned in and lamented, "Anna Gonzales. She used to be a student here, but she's been missing now for about a year. Tragic, really."

"What happened to her?"

Ms. Walker shrugged. "We've looked everywhere on the island for her. Mr. Alderman even paid for the search. I pray she just got on a boat and left St. Thomas rather than somewhere out there."

Jimmy watched Ms. Walker's watering eyes gaze out the window into the endless Caribbean Sea in front of them.

"She was a great athlete," Ms. Walker said, studying the team basketball photo in the next cabinet.

"Who's that right next to her?" Jimmy asked. It was her. The girl he'd driven to the island. Monica.

"Monica Diaz," Ms. Walker said. "Anna and Monica were best friends. After Anna disappeared, Monica took it the hardest."

"Where is she now, Monica?"

"She comes in once in a while but then disappears again."

Jimmy did the math in his head. "When was the last time she was here?"

"Two weeks ago, I think."

"Thanks for everything, Ms. Walker," Jimmy said.

"Absolutely, anything to help Mr. Alderman," Ms. Walker responded. "Wait, I didn't even get your name?"

"Um...James."

Before she could respond, Jimmy was out the door.

23

When Jimmy returned from Charlotte Amalie, island nightlife had consumed Red Hook. Music rumbled from the Crab Shack, and tourists spilled along the quaint downtown street. It was business as usual.

Jimmy buzzed through. He was tired and wanted to get home. He had had a long enough day. Now that he knew the truth about The Freedom Dove House, he would find Eddie tomorrow and make him come clean. Tell him everything.

After Jimmy made it through downtown the road returned to the quiet darkness of unlit island streets.

Glare from the car headlights behind him reflected in Jimmy's side mirror. Jimmy squinted. He despised it when people used their high beams on these poor roads.

Suddenly the car sped up and was directly on his bumper. It was the same black Range Rover SUV that had trailed him the other day. The engine revved and came inches from the back of his Vespa.

Jimmy knew he was dead if he fell.

Sweat trickled down his face; someone was trying to kill him. He turned the throttle on the small moped. His speed barely picked up. The old Vespa could only handle so much.

The SUV rushed forward again.

There were so many crashes on these dark roads. It would be easy to write off Jimmy's death as an accident.

Jimmy swerved, and the Range Rover passed by.

Jimmy slowed and moved the Vespa to the edge of the road as quickly as possible. If he stayed on the road any longer, whoever was doing this would try again.

Jimmy caught his breath once he was safely on the curb.

The Range Rover jammed on its brakes, leaving a patch of rubber on the road. The three-ton SUV swiftly turned around and accelerated toward Jimmy.

Headlights blinded Jimmy as the car shot at him. He froze. He thought about diving into the jungle brush, but the growth was too far.

Jimmy tensed and shielded himself from impact.

Suddenly the Range Rover skidded to a standstill a few feet from Jimmy. The rich blue halogen lights jerking to a halt.

Jimmy gasped a whisper of relief.

The driver's side door of the SUV opened. A figure stepped out. Shadowed by the headlights, Jimmy couldn't make out any details.

"Where is she?" The voice was rough and unfamil-iar.

"Who?" Jimmy shouted. He was nervous, but now that this son-of-a-bitch was out of his SUV Jimmy stood a chance.

"The girl." The man cracked his knuckles and marched toward Jimmy. His stance like a linebacker and his frame like a bodybuilder.

"Fuck you!" Jimmy yelled.

Jimmy stood in a fighting stance, preparing for a right hook from the man. The figure swung. A left hook cracked Jimmy in the jaw.

Dazed, Jimmy stiffened up. This guy was a fighter. Jimmy swung and missed. He felt another punch to his abdomen, instantly bringing Jimmy to his knees. The man lined up like he was punting a football and kicked Jimmy in the ribs.

The next thing Jimmy knew, he was on his back, staring up at the stars.

"Where is the girl?" the man said as he applied pressure on Jimmy's chest with his foot.

Jimmy tried to breathe. Pain burned through his chest. "I don't know," he winced.

The man took his heel off Jimmy's ribs and said, "I know where you live. I can get to you anytime. Next time I won't be so lovely."

In the dim light of the Ranger Rover headlights, Jimmy noticed the man wore wing-tipped shoes. Jimmy tried his best to breathe as the memories flashed through his mind. He had seen those shoes before, but where?

Jimmy leaned back on the asphalt. It was still warm from soaking up the sun's rays all day. The man with the wing-tipped shoes got in the Range Rover and drove away, leaving Jimmy alone in the dark on the side of the street.

Those wing-tipped shoes jogged Jimmy's memory. He had seen those shoes before but couldn't place them. Finally, Ramirez and his massive frame flashed across Jimmy's mind. He had noticed Ramirez wearing those same shoes the night he had dropped Monica off at Little Saint George.

Jimmy gradually got to his feet. He tasted blood, but he knew this little visit had been a warning. If they had wanted him dead, it would have been easy. Jimmy wasn't shocked that Alderman's goons were behind this. They must have been worried about his visit to The Freedom Dove House. He was on to something.

Fifteen minutes later, Jimmy drove the Vespa into the Dive Shop lot. His head still throbbed, his side hurt. He had ripped off the sleeve of his shirt to stop the bleeding on the cut above his eye.

After parking his moped, he walked to the cooler, pulled out a cold Bud Light, and used it as an ice pack against his eye. He was in over his head. Of course, Alderman was going to keep an eye on him.

Jimmy made a whiskey on ice and twirled the dark liquid under the moonlight. The sound of ice tingling against the side of the glass relaxed him. The burn of the whiskey down his throat was bliss. Numbness followed. He was almost there. He poured another drink, lit a cigarette, and with a thump fell into his beach chair.

Everything hurt, but no bones were broken. The pain didn't bother him. For some twisted reason, it exhilarated him, made him feel alive. Jimmy didn't want to add Monica Diaz's face to that list of kids he could have saved. If that meant a little blood spilled on his behalf, he would gladly do it. Regrettably, Jimmy assumed the worst for Anna Gonzalez. Why else would he have discovered her necklace at the bottom of the ocean? He prayed he wasn't too late for Monica.

"James?" a sultry voice said from the dark.

Jimmy clutched his chest and practically fell out of the rusty beach chair.

Lisa Brenner walked out of the dark wearing a skin-tight black dress. Her brunette hair shoulder-length, her skin a golden brown. She looked sexy as hell. Jimmy knew she wanted something from him and he was in no condition to refuse.

24

"Were you waiting in the dark, watching me?"

Lisa Brenner tilted her head like it was no big deal.

"James, did you get in an accident? You look hurt," Lisa's voice was soft and caring, but Jimmy didn't trust her.

Jimmy adjusted the cold beer over his injury. "Something like that."

"You should be more careful?"

"I should be more careful?" Jimmy squirmed in his chair. "What have you got me mixed up in? I just got attacked by one of Alderman's henchmen. It seems like your fake daughter is popular."

"I'm sorry, James. I didn't mean for this to happen to you." Lisa grabbed a bar rag off the table and submerged it in the ice cooler. She strolled toward Jimmy and wiped the dried blood off his face.

Jimmy winced.

"Did you learn anything about her?" Lisa removed one of Jimmy's cigarettes out of his breast pocket and lifted an eyebrow. She wanted a light.

Jimmy reached into his pocket for his lighter and cringed. His ribs hurt.

"Have you ever heard of the Freedom Dove House?" Jimmy asked and lit her cigarette. "It's a shelter for trafficked young girls?"

Lisa exhaled, "No." The smoke swirled out of her plump lips. She wore strawberry-red lipstick.

"Well, it's one of Alderman's charities."

Lisa refilled Jimmy's whiskey and asked, "What does this have to do with the girl?"

The cold brown liquid baked Jimmy's throat like swallowing a fireball. He felt loose and ready to chat.

"She was a student there. Monica Diaz, that's her real name. Alderman's got the girls working all over the island. He calls it a 'work-study program,'" Jimmy rolled his eyes, "But something tells me he doesn't have them just changing sheets and making coffee, if you know what I mean."

Jimmy could tell Lisa understood.

"But how do you know for sure?" Lisa replied.

"I went to the island yesterday."

"You what? You met with Alderman?" Lisa appeared annoyed.

"Yes. He tried to buy me off. Get me to give up the investigation." Jimmy paused and lit another cigarette, "Well, I guess he did buy me off, because I took the money, but those are just minor details."

"Why did you do that? He is a dangerous man. He has connections all over the world: the CIA, Israeli intelligence. You saw the people that were at Cyber Talks."

"Like your husband?"

"My husband is dead."

The grieving widow routine wasn't working on Jimmy anymore. Every politician appreciates a good sob story, and Lisa Brenner had been in the business long enough.

Jimmy adjusted himself in the chair. "Let me ask you this: where were you the night he died?"

Lisa stepped back, "Are you serious?"

Jimmy was serious. "You know the investigation into his death is still ongoing, right?"

"Who did you talk to?" Lisa asked.

Jimmy could tell Lisa wasn't convinced.

"The police said your husband hit his head before he drowned."

"I told you, the girl—Monica— she had something to do with it."

"The mysterious girl we can't find?"

"The mysterious girl you drove to the island that killed my husband?"

"Okay, fine," Jimmy didn't want to argue anymore.

He doubted Monica had anything to do with the murder. Alderman and his associates, on the other hand, were the prime suspects. Jimmy was still interested in what Lisa's connection to him was.

"What's your relationship with Alderman?"

Jimmy was prepared for another argument when he asked that question, but her reaction surprised him.

Lisa Brenner exhaled and sat in one of the empty beach chairs and said, "I think I'll have that drink now."

Jimmy got up, made her a cocktail, and freshened up his. Whiskey on the rocks—guaranteed to numb any pain.

Lisa took a sip. She wasn't a whiskey drinker, but she drank it anyway.

"Jonathan financed William's career right from the first time he ran for Senator up to his Presidential run." Lisa took a sip. She was getting used to the whiskey. "I remember we all met at his house in Aspen to discuss the Presidential race. It was perfect— logs burning in his massive fireplace. We were so excited about the future. We thought he had a chance."

Lisa finished her whiskey. "Well, you know how the story ended. Five months later, 'Babysitter-Gate,' and like that, it was over."

"Front page of every newspaper in the Virgin Islands, so that means it was everywhere stateside," Jimmy said. He remembered making jokes about it with Kate when it happened.

"All of his support dried up overnight, then Jonathan threw his support and money behind someone else."

"Why did you stay with him?"

Lisa shrugged and poured another drink, "the media and newspapers liked to speculate that I was a victim in all of this—and I was to a certain extent, but we both had separate lives outside of our public image."

"Affairs?"

"I'm not an angel, if that's what you're asking."

Jimmy knew not to pry. Everyone has secrets.

"What happened between your husband and Alderman?"

Lisa let out a sigh. "Good thing he had two years before his Senate reelection. It allowed things to die down. I supported my husband, but Jonathan didn't. William gave that race everything he had, and the only way to win back that seat was to go his own way. Jonathan didn't like that."

Then it all came to Jimmy. At the Cyber Talks conference, Jimmy remembered how Brenner faced all those boos from the audience. They seemed to hate him for what he said.

"The Internet Freedom Act?" Jimmy said.

Lisa nodded. "I thought attending the conference was going to help William and Jonathan rebuild their relationship, but William said he would never vote for it no matter what Alderman gave him."

"Do you think Alderman had something to do with his death?"

"He's not stupid."

"You know he's searching for the girl too?" Jimmy rubbed his head. He still had a headache.

"We have to find her before they do."

Lisa got out of her chair and walked toward Jimmy and said, "You might have a concussion."

"I'm fine." Jimmy took a sip of whiskey.

Lisa dipped the rag in the cooler, sat on Jimmy's lap, and wiped his face. She straddled him. He could feel her inner thigh through her skirt. He knew she could feel how hard he was.

"If you don't want to talk about it—that's fine." She dabbed the cold rag on his forehead.

Jimmy felt better. Perhaps it was the whiskey, but he knew it was the beautiful woman in front of him.

"Life is full of regrets," he said, "and I have mine."

"We all do," Lisa whispered in his ear. Her lips were soft and moist when she kissed him.

Jimmy thought of all those kids he could have saved. "Sometimes you fuck up the past so much there's no going back."

"All you can do is move forward." Lisa kissed him again.

Jimmy slid his hands down Lisa's back; the outline of her lace panties weakened him. He wanted her and pulled her closer. She was the only thing that made him feel good inside.

Jimmy took her on the dock, but all he could think about was that island in the distance. Something was going on there, and he was going to find out even if it killed him.

25

The next day all that remained of Lisa Brenner was the faint smell of her perfume on Jimmy's shirt. He vaguely remembered feeling her lips against his right before she left, but he wasn't sure. He could have dreamt it.

After a shower and light breakfast of coffee and cigarette's, Jimmy was on the road toward Red Hook to find Eddie and finally get some answers.

Jimmy's first stop was Marooned.

As he wound along the secluded island road, he thought of Lisa. She was a mystery to him. He knew she was using him, but to what end? Maybe it didn't matter; he didn't mind being used by a beautiful woman.

Jimmy pulled off the small island road onto the freshly paved asphalt of the main road to downtown Red Hook. A glint forty yards behind him caught his eye. He glanced in the rearview mirror and noticed the same black SUV from last night.

They must have been waiting for him. It was broad daylight. There was no way anyone would try and do anything to him now.

The modest tires of the Vespa scooter shot up small stones and pebbles as the moped took off. Jimmy knew he didn't have much time if he wanted to lose the SUV. If Eddie did have answers, Jimmy didn't want to bring heat onto him. A bend in the road up ahead and some heavy ferns would give Jimmy some shelter to hide, but he had to be quick. The SUV was already after him.

Jimmy swiftly rounded the curve and turned the moped at a 90 degree angle. He thrust his foot on the ground, worried he might fall and skin his legs on the road. He tried his best to keep his balance. Jimmy turned the throttle on full again and shot into the thick ferns on the side of the road.

Jimmy had used this hiding spot in the past to retrieve coke and other uppers and downers to sell to tourists. Jimmy skidded the motorbike to a stop. He promptly got off and ran back toward the road to see if he could get a good glimpse at the SUV driver through the ferns. Krauthammer was behind the wheel. His eyes scanned the jungle.

Jimmy waited patiently in the hiding spot, watching Krauthammer drive the SUV up and down the road. After about an hour, Jimmy figured Krauthammer had given up. Jimmy rolled the Vespa out of the ferns, then continued on his way to the Marooned Bar.

The bar was quiet. It was still morning. The regulars were at home recovering from the night before. But that didn't matter to Jimmy. He only needed to talk to one person.

Jimmy marched down the narrow dock. Eddie was sitting at the end, silhouetted by the morning sun. He fiddled with his phone while smoking a joint and listening to ear pods.

"Where is she?" Jimmy demanded. He tapped Eddie on the shoulder, who promptly pulled off his ear pods. Jimmy could tell Eddie was startled.

"A little jumpy, huh?" Jimmy asked. "Something wrong?"

"Nah, man." Eddie laughed nervously. "What are you doing here?"

"Eddie," Jimmy was stern, "where is she?"

"Huh?"

"Monica Diaz?" Jimmy could feel the cop part of him that had laid dormant for so long begin to come to the surface. It felt good.

"Who?"

"Look, I know about the Freedom Dove House, the island, Alderman," Jimmy spoke softer. He needed Eddie to trust him, and know he was there to help. "I'm her only hope. Alderman is after her, and it will be a matter of time before the police think she had something to do with Senator Brenner's death."

Eddie threw the butt of his joint in the ocean and squirmed in his beach chair.

"She had nothing to do with it." Eddie was defensive.

"I know." Jimmy put up his hands, trying to reassure him.

"You don't understand, man. They're watching every move I make. I can't make a move. They're everywhere."

Jimmy figured as much from Eddie's reaction. He was being followed as well, yet Jimmy needed more information if he was going to help. "How do you know her?" Jimmy said.

Eddie glanced around out of habit. There was no one there. Jimmy understood Eddie was in some serious shit. "I met her at the Crab Shack a while back," Eddie muttered. His hand trembled as he put his phone back in his pocket. "She made me promise not to tell anybody what happens on that island. She said it's dangerous."

"It's dangerous now, Eddie," Jimmy responded. "I don't think you realize how big this goes."

"I realize how big this goes," Eddie shouted, then caught his voice and returned to a whisper. "That's why I'm scared shitless, and you should be too."

"It's only a matter of time until they find her. Where is she? I can help."

Eddie sank back in his chair and took a breath. His eyes swelled with water, but no tears fell. "I don't know what to do with her. Alderman is connected everywhere on this island and beyond. I'm talking about our government, foreign governments, you should hear the stories I've heard. It's fuckin' unbelievable. Hell, I didn't believe it at first."

"I believe you." Jimmy knew this was big.

Eddie ran his sweaty hand through his hair then nodded in the direction of the thick jungle area on the other side of the razor wire fence enclosing the property.

Jimmy lifted his head and peered in the direction Eddie pointed. The boat graveyard was the adjoining property. Beyond the razor wire fence and dense jungle vegetation, hundreds of fractured, broken masses and the corpses of old rusted boats lay decaying, like neglected remains in a muddy mass grave.

Monica Diaz was somewhere in that landfill, and Jimmy knew that's where he had to go.

26

The rain clouds above began to spit. Jimmy followed Eddie down the dock and toward the razor wire fence. The soil was dark and damp, but Jimmy could tell Eddie had traversed this path before by the way he stepped on stable stones to keep his feet dry. After a few minutes of Jimmy using his arms to block the incoming ferns from snapping back into his face, they made it to the old fence.

Rusted razor wire wrapped the chain-link fence like shark teeth. There was no way they were going to hop it without serious injury.

"This way," Eddie whispered and motioned along the fence exterior. Cut into the side was a small hole. Eddie squeezed through, and Jimmy followed.

The boat graveyard was just that—a cemetery. Deteriorating boats peppered the muddy ground. Shards of glass and serrated steel jumbled the slender dirt path that snaked between the vessels.

Rain fell harder. Mud oozed around Jimmy's toes with every step. Jimmy's flip flops were not thick enough to stop whatever contaminated the terrain from touching his skin.

"I was the one who picked her up from the island that night," Eddie whispered. He pushed aside some vines expanding across the path like a spiderweb.

"Let me guess," Jimmy said. "You used my boat?"

Eddie laughed. "I would have asked, but you were blackout drunk."

"Well, I can't fault you for that. At least you drove me home after. You bring Monica right here after you got her back to St. Thomas?"

"Yes. I knew Alderman was going to be searching for her. He owns the cops. I didn't know what else to do."

"Weren't you worried about if the cameras spotted you? Alderman has them everywhere on the island."

"Not where I picked her up. Monica was careful. She knew the island well."

A few moments later, Eddie stopped in front of one of the boat wrecks. An old fishing boat, nearly thirty feet long with a small cabin. The hull was a discolored blue and yellowing white. Torn through the stern, a massive hole from god-knows-what clearly indicated why the vessel was discarded here.

Jimmy brushed the dirt off the small cabin window. A cloth or shade immediately moved inside.

"She in there?" Jimmy asked. He knew she was but wanted Eddie to speak.

Eddie stared at the marshy soil and squished a piece of cement into the mud. "I didn't know where else to hide her."

"I have a few ideas," Jimmy said. He wiped the rain off his face; his clothes were thoroughly soaked. "Are we going to do this, or are we just going to stand in the rain like a couple of idiots?"

Eddie glanced up and exhaled, then knocked on the boat hull. "It's Eddie. I'm coming up, and I brought help."

Jimmy followed Eddie over a few empty oil drums that acted as stairs into the back of the fishing boat. The vessel wobbled on its concrete stilts for a second as the two men climbed in and then settled back into the mud.

Moss and patches of mushrooms grew on parts of the boat interior that still had access to the elements. Part of the seat cushion head had been chewed and ripped out. A rat scurried across the floor and hastily exited through a crack in the hull. Jimmy cautiously made his way toward the cabin. The last thing he wanted to do was slip, break a leg, or get tetanus. Jimmy opened the cabin hatch.

The room was dim and musty. A half-eaten pizza was on the table. Thin slits of light cut across the small room, lighting the face of a girl. Scared and curled up in the corner, she held a knife securely in her hand. She pointed it at Jimmy.

The girl was Monica Diaz.

She was terrified, like a battered dog in the corner of a kennel. A thin layer of grime covered her skin; her hair was knotted and unwashed. Jimmy didn't want to startle her any more than she already was.

"Do you remember me?" Jimmy whispered. He offered her his hand.

Monica nodded her head YES, however, she didn't put down the knife.

"I want to help you," Jimmy said.

Monica straightened out the knife and chewed on the corner of her mouth. She wasn't going anywhere.

Jimmy recognized she needed time to consider her options; nevertheless, they still needed to move quickly. It would only be a matter of time before Krauthammer came to the Marooned Bar looking for Eddie. If Jimmy found the pieces to put the puzzle together, they would too.

"You can trust him," Eddie chimed. His reassuring voice came from behind Jimmy.

"You can keep the knife," Jimmy said. He wanted her to feel safe. "But we have to get you out of here."

Monica shook her head. "No. Alderman knows people everywhere."

"I know, Monica, but you're not safe here either. If I found you, it's only a matter of time before they do. Please," Jimmy insisted.

Thunder exploded from above and shuddered the ship. Jimmy stabled himself on the side of the entrance. Rain fell harder and began flooding into the boat like a river.

"I want to help," he said again.

Jimmy reached into his pocket and removed the dove pendant.

"This is Anna Gonzalez's, right?"

Monica nodded.

"And that's why you went to island, to figure out what happened to her?"

"Yes."

"And Brenner was your only way on the island?"

"Yes."

"The girl with the pink streak in her hair told you what happened to Anna, right?"

Monica dropped the knife and started to sob. "I don't know where to go. They'll kill me just like they killed her."

Jimmy reached out his hand. "I know a place where you'll be safe."

Monica glanced up. Her makeup still smudged from the night Jimmy drove her to the island. She clasped the dove pendant which still draped around her neck, and took Jimmy's hand.

"I trust you."

27

Curtis Blue arrived at the junkyard once night came. He had gone to school with the guy who owned it. Rusty was his name, and he didn't give a shit about what they were doing. Curtis brought him some jerk-chicken, and Rusty stayed inside the office watching football.

Curtis backed his beat-up Toyota pickup truck into the junkyard. Jimmy acted as lookout just in case there were wandering eyes from other employees. But it was dark, still pouring rain. Nobody wanted to go outside.

Jimmy and Eddie quickly moved Monica to the back of the pickup truck. Eddie jumped in, and Jimmy threw an old tarp over the two of them. The tarp was filthy, and there were enough holes to still get them wet, but it did the trick. They were hidden.

Jimmy jumped in the cab with Curtis and said, "I owe you. Curtis, this is huge."

Curtis nodded his head and lit the joint dangling from his lips. Jimmy knew he understood. They pulled out of the boat graveyard. Jimmy could still see Rusty and his guys watching TV and eating chicken through the window. They hadn't seen a thing.

When they passed Marooned, Jimmy quickly got out and loaded his Vespa in the back. He strapped it in the back of the truck so it wouldn't slide on Monica and Eddie as the truck moved.

The two men were silent for the next few minutes until they were safely down the street. Jimmy looked back. He didn't see anyone following them. Jimmy exhaled, and for the next twenty minutes, Jimmy told Curtis everything that had happened.

By the time they got to the safe house up in the hills, the rain had stopped. With one massive tug, Jimmy pulled the tarp off of Monica and Eddie. They cuddled in the bed of the truck, Eddie's arms wrapped around Monica like a protector. Jimmy could tell this experience had brought them closer together. Eddie was a good kid, and she needed his support now.

"You can stay here as long as you want," Curtis said.

Eddie helped Monica out of the back of the truck, careful not to slip in the muddy puddles that had formed.

"It's my sister's place," Curtis continued, "and she lives in the States now."

Monica looked up. Nestled in the side of the jungle was a small house. She then glanced from Curtis to Jimmy, and then to Eddie and said, "Thank you."

Eddie grasped her hand. "You'll be safe here."

"You're leaving?" Monica said.

"I have to get back. If I don't show my face people will start asking questions, you know? I'll be back after my shift."

Monica hugged Eddie.

"Be careful," she said. "You know what they can do. I can't lose you too."

Eddie kissed her and smiled. "You won't lose me." Eddie turned to Curtis and Jimmy. "Whatever I can do, let me know."

"She's in good hands," Jimmy said. "We'll keep her safe."

The safehouse was quaint. It had one floor and was on a slab on concrete, nothing fancy but much better than the boat—no rats or bugs. The living room was pleasant, with a big puffy couch. The wall to the kitchen had been knocked down at one point, making the house seem bigger than it actually was.

"The bathroom and shower are through there," Curtis said, pointing to the only room other than the kitchen and living room. "My sister is about your size, or was when she lived here. You'll find some clothes in the closet.

Monica thanked Curtis then went into the bedroom to clean up. Jimmy waited until the bedroom door locked and Monica turned on the shower before he spoke.

"I have to get her off the island."

"Jimbo, this is serious shit." Curtis braced himself on the kitchen counter as he spoke. "Alderman is connected all the way. What if he finds her?"

"I don't know," Jimmy said, lowering his voice. "The Senator is dead, Anna Gonzalez is missing, probably dead." Jimmy showed Curtis the pendant. "I found this diving. You can hide a lot of secrets under the water."

Curtis looked at the pendant then handed it back. "You go to the police?"

"I don't trust them. What about Douglas? I know it's a long shot, but maybe he can help."

"Don't know, brotha. Douglas don't want this type of attention. But she's safe here until we find plan B. This road is quiet. No one comes up here."

Curtis handed Jimmy the key and left with Eddie.

Thirty minutes later, Monica stepped out of the bedroom. Her hair was still damp from the shower.

"Smells good," she said.

Jimmy was cooking a fried egg over rice, one of his favorite meals. "I'll pick something fancier up tomorrow, muffins or something like that."

"This is fine." She smiled. "Coffee?"

Jimmy moved out of the way, revealing a pot of coffee. "Can't forget that. Cream or sugar?"

"No, thanks."

"All natural. Black. The best way to drink it."

Jimmy poured her a cup and refilled his.

For the next few minutes, Jimmy watched Monica scarf down her breakfast. She must have been starving. You can only live off stale pizza for so long. Jimmy filled her plate with a second helping, then leaned against the kitchen countertop, replaying the events of the past few days in his head.

He was relieved that he'd gotten her out of the boat graveyard, but he knew she was still in danger. Ramirez and Krauthammer were probably combing the whole island for her. With Alderman's money, they had unlimited resources. Jimmy didn't know what his next move was.

"You ever thought about going back to the Freedom Dove House?" Jimmy broke the silence. "They could help, right?"

Monica washed her final mouthful of food down with coffee. "Too dangerous. They have cameras everywhere, and Alderman pays them enough money to look the other way."

Jimmy reached his hand into his pocket and hesitated for a second, then pulled out the pendant.

"I think you should have this."

Monica took the pendant.

"You know, Anna used to work on the island doing whatever Mr. Alderman asked." Monica swallowed hard. "That night when I saw you with her necklace, and you said you found it in the water, I knew right there what had happened."

Monica held back tears. "I pictured her at the bottom of the ocean, alone, with...things, sea creatures crawling all over her." She shivered. "I almost didn't get on the boat. It was stupid of me. I should have just gotten on a plane to Miami and just disappeared."

"You're safe now," Jimmy reassured her.

Monica's shoulders tensed. Jimmy could tell she wasn't convinced. "People like Alderman always seem to get away."

The way Monica said it struck him. It was like a forgone conclusion that Alderman was untouchable, like he was from a protected class of people.

"Not this time," Jimmy said with certainty. Anger bubbled up inside him. Jimmy's stomach churned at the thought of Alderman getting away with what he'd done. It made him nauseous, furious. At that moment, Jimmy knew he would do anything to make sure Alderman got his due.

"Did you call the police?" Monica asked.

"Not yet," Jimmy said. He needed more information before he made his next move. He wanted to be sure how deep this went, and who the players were.

Jimmy refilled their coffee.

"What about the other girls on the island?" he asked. "The ones who cleaned the sheets, made the beds, that type of thing."

"He used them just like me. He uses everyone, twisting and manipulating people so he can control them. He would find your weakness and then exploit that. Powerful people from around the world, who think they're above consequence, Alderman controlled them too." Monica glanced up. Her eyes cold and serious. "Sex is everyone's weakness."

"And the Senator?" Jimmy asked.

Monica adjusted herself in her chair. "That night was different. Mr. Alderman wanted a girl from off the island. He wanted me to look mature. Carmen knew I wanted to get on the island, so she suggested me. She got me on the guest list."

"Carmen?" Jimmy said. "The girl with the pink streak in her hair?"

"Yes."

"What happened the night Senator Brenner died?"

"I didn't know he was going to die." Monica started to cry. It was the first time she seemed her age: Monica Diaz, a sixteen-year-old girl. "I swear," Monica pleaded, "I didn't have anything to do with it."

"I know," Jimmy said. His voice was soft and comforting. The training he'd had as a cop was still there.

"They just came in," Monica continued, crying now. "I saw it. I saw everything. I knew I had to hide, or I would end up like Anna."

"You're not going to end up like her," Jimmy insisted.

Monica took a deep breath and began to describe the night Senator Brenner died.

28

"Is that the Senator?" Monica asked Carmen, the pink-haired girl in the island polo shirt. The two girls huddled together at the edge of the amphitheater.

Senator Brenner bellowed from the Cyber Talks stage about some Internet Act that Monica had no clue about.

"Yes," said Carmen. "That's him. You know what you're supposed to do?"

Monica nodded. She was nervous.

"Bungalow seven," Carmen whispered.

Out of the corner of Monica's eye, she saw Jimmy. The boat driver who had brought her to the island. He was glancing around the amphitheater, probably looking for her. Monica quickly moved behind Carmen, so she was out of his sight. She didn't want anything else to do with the boat driver. What was he doing here, anyway? He was supposed to stay in the boat.

"Who is that guy?" Carmen asked.

"Nobody," Monica quickly said. She didn't want to get Jimmy in any more trouble than he already was.

Suddenly Monica saw one of the big guys from the dock grab Jimmy from behind and drag him toward the exit. Jimmy kicked and shouted, but his efforts were drowned out by the noise of the speakers.

Monica felt bad, but she was relieved Jimmy was gone. He wasn't a bad guy, just pathetic.

When the Senator finished his speech, Monica promptly exited the amphitheater to wait for Brenner at bungalow seven. The roar of the theater was soon replaced by the quiet sound of crickets as she made her way along the limestone walkway.

Monica's heart raced with nervous excitement as she moved through the freshly landscaped ground. The spill of light from the amphitheater receded, and now she was guided by tiki torches and the moonlight. She felt powerful, like she was in command. She loathed these men, all of them, but her disgust made her feel strong.

Inside the bungalow, she adjusted herself in the mirror and gulped a large swig of champagne from the uncorked bottle to take the edge off. She knew they were watching, listening.

Moments later, a soft knock tapped on the door. Senator Brenner strolled in. He was tall and sturdy like a police officer from the old movies. Monica felt confident and ready. She approached him, grabbed him by the hand, and led him toward the bed.

Afterward, dread replaced Monica's sense of power and excitement. What had she done? There were other ways to make money. Senator Brenner stood naked in front of her. His skin sagged off his bones, his teeth yellowing. Brenner picked his pants up off the floor and pulled out five one-hundred-dollar bills. He laid them on the bed.

Monica felt nauseous, dirty. She turned her back toward the Senator as she put her dress back on. Monica was guilty too. She wasn't as powerful as she'd thought. Monica wanted to get out as quickly as possible. She had learned what happened to Anna. It was time to go.

"What is this?" the Senator said. His tone baffled as if caught off guard.

Monica turned around, alarmed. Brenner squinted at the wall next to the mirror as if he was inspecting something. His face no further than an inch from the cedar wood casing.

Monica feared the worst. She didn't want a part of this anymore. She wanted to leave, though Brenner blocked the exit.

The Senator continued scratching the wall, then something snapped off, and he removed the miniature camera lodged inside the wood.

"This better not be what I think it is," the Senator said. He was angry now. Furious. He threw it on the floor and crunched it beneath the heel of his foot.

Brenner lunged at Monica and, frozen in fear, Monica couldn't move. He grabbed her by the arm. It ached. It was harder than anyone had seized her before.

"Did you know about this?" the Senator roared. His face so close she could feel the warmth from his breath.

Terrified, Monica couldn't speak.

"Say something, dammit!"

"They made me do it," Monica muttered. She shielded her eyes. She couldn't look him in the face. His was bitter and contorted, like a monster.

"Who?" Brenner squeezed her harder.

Monica attempted to pull away, but couldn't. Her arm burned. "You're hurting me," she winced.

Brenner's eyes darted around the room. "Are there other cameras in here?"

Monica nodded her head. She knew all the places where Alderman hid cameras.

Monica glanced at the mirror.

Brenner charged toward the mirror, dragging Monica by the arm. He ripped it off the wall. The mirror shattered on impact, pieces of glasses just missing her feet. Concealed behind the mirror was a second camera.

Brenner glared at Monica. "Have you done this before?"

She had, "I'm sorry."

"Was it Alderman?"

Brenner let go of Monica and yelled, "Where are you, Alderman? Is this how you get what you want?"

Monica knew Alderman heard Brenner. She was sure there were other cameras in the room, and now that Brenner was exposed, Alderman would arrive soon.

Brenner flipped over the mattress and ripped pictures off the walls. Monica knew this was her only chance to get away. Occupied trying to find the other cameras, Brenner wasn't paying attention to her.

Go now, she thought.

Monica darted across the room, grabbed her shoes, and left the bungalow.

It was so dark outside she couldn't see well. Suddenly up ahead, she overheard voices and saw three silhouettes walking toward the bungalow. Monica sprinted to the backside of the cabin and hid in the ferns behind.

She closed her eyes and prayed that no one saw her. It was never supposed to go this way. In and out, she was told, then quickly leave. She heard the three figures getting closer.

The sound of soft footsteps on the grass turned into taps on wood. They were inside the bungalow.

"You son of a bitch!" Monica heard Senator Brenner yell from inside the bungalow.

Monica was curious. She hunched down and crawled toward the bungalow.

"You've always had a weakness for the flesh," a nasally voice responded.

The voice sounded familiar, but Monica couldn't place it.

"Is this what you do?" Brenner shot back. "Blackmail people into whatever you want?"

Monica crept closer to the window. The ground was soft beneath her legs. She wanted to look inside and see. She had to.

Monica lifted her head and looked inside.

Dressed in a tan linen suit with a white t-shirt underneath, Alderman stood on the opposite side of the room from where Brenner was. Two massive men stood on either side of Alderman like Roman pillars. Their faces hard, one like a pit-bull, the other like a slab of concrete.

They were the men from the dock.

"Where is the girl?" Alderman snapped.

Fear gripped Monica. Her hands began to sweat; she had to get off the island.

29

"I know what you want," Brenner yelled at Alderman. "You want me to change my vote. Never. Blackmailing a politician for this kind of shit doesn't hold weight anymore. No one gives a shit. You can't do anything to me that hasn't already been done."

Brenner put his sport coat back on and snapped it taut to get all the wrinkles out. "Plus, Lisa knows who I am, what I do. And trust me, she's no saint either. This little incident won't even make the news."

Alderman smirked. "That's true you and your wife have a peculiar arrangement, and you're right, society has grown more liberal on some issues. A philandering husband, a promiscuous wife. But that's not the whole story, William. Here's where it gets a little interesting."

"What are you talking about?" Brenner responded.

Alderman pointed at one of the cameras in the wall hanging by a wire and raised an eyebrow. "I knew you liked them young William, but not that young."

Brenner's brow furrowed. "What are you talking about?

Monica continued to watch the interaction between the men. She knew the implications of Brenner sleeping with an underage girl, her. But Monica didn't care. It was just sex to her, and money. However, watching the blackmail part gave the situation a realness she had never experienced before. She felt terrible for him.

"She's sixteen, William." Alderman added, "Now your tombstone will read: 'Presidential prospect, political counter-culture icon, and your average penitentiary pedophile.'"

Brenner paused. His shoulders slumped.

"No, no," Brenner repeated. Monica could tell he was scared. "That will never happen," he exclaimed. "You sent her to me. She was on your island."

"There's no record of her working here, William." Alderman was calm and methodical with his words.

"I know your secrets, too," Brenner bellowed at Alderman. "What goes on here, on this island. All I have to do is leak it to the press, and you're finished."

Alderman smiled and shook his head. "Do you think people are going to believe you? Actors, politicians, Presidents, royalty all come here; they're not going to let you destroy all they've built. These people don't want their private life out in the open like that. They want to make movies, run countries, get awards, just like you."

Brenner pleaded. "You would destroy me, Jonathan? After all we have been through?"

"Of course not, William. I don't want to destroy you." Alderman moved closer and put his arm around Brenner's shoulder. "You can still be an icon. Hell, you could even run for President again. People love second chances; a comeback is an American tradition. I want to see you succeed. And the girl? She's cute, sexy. It could happen to anyone. And if you liked her, we can get her back for you. Or you can pick whatever girl you see here." Alderman pointed at the cameras and then waved them away. "We can pretend this never happened. No one ever needs to see the video."

"How do I know you won't release the tapes after I do what you want?"

"Because it doesn't benefit me, William. I like you. I like your wife, your family. That's who you have to think about."

Brenner exhaled. "And what if I don't?"

Alderman glanced at the two men next to him. "There's a long line of people who want to be a US Senator. The ocean is big, William."

"Are you saying what I think you're saying?"

Monica could tell Brenner was getting angry now.

Alderman cocked his head and shrugged.

"That's what I thought you said," Brenner suddenly pulled out a pistol, surprising Alderman and the men next to him.

"Wait a minute," Alderman said, and backed up to the door.

"You can't push me around. I'm a fuckin' US Senator, for Christ's sake. You've fucked with me too much. Your gonna take me to your little command center here so I can see the tape. I want it destroyed in front of my own eyes."

"I can't do that," Alderman said, calmly shaking his head back and forth.

Brenner straightened the pistol. "Oh yes, you will. I'm not leaving this place until you do."

Suddenly one of the big men lunged at Brenner. The gun exploded, a blast of fire erupted from the tip of the weapon. Blood splattered over the mirror. Monica couldn't tell whose blood it was, but she was sure someone was shot. One of the big men seemed to collapse on top of Brenner, like a football player sacking the quarterback. Alderman escaped to the corner of the room. The second big man pulled a pistol from his coat.

Monica ducked her head below the window; she feared Alderman or one of his men would see her. Moans came from the bungalow floor, but Monica couldn't tell if it was Brenner or the big guy that had fallen on top of him.

There was a long pause before Monica heard Alderman say, "Is he dead?"

Monica stopped. She wanted to flee, but had to see. She had to be sure who was dead. Monica slowly lifted her head and peeked in the window. Alderman and the other man, now clutching the arm bleeding from the gunshot, looked down at Brenner's lifeless body. The third man was on his knees, checking Brenner's pulse.

"He fuckin' shot me," one of the men said. "I can't believe he fuckin' shot me." The man clutched his arm. Blood had soaked through his suit coat, but it was difficult to see in the dark.

"There's nothing. No pulse," the man replied. "He must have smacked his head on the corner of the table."

Monica glanced at Brenner. Blood pooled around his head near the floor of the glass end table that had shattered. On Brenner's face, an expression of astonishment, like even he was surprised he was dead. His eyes rolled back, and his mouth opened.

"What do we do?" Alderman asked. A level of concern audible in his voice.

The man with the pit-bull face tightened the grip on his arm and said, "We get rid of him. Take him to the ocean. He's been drinking, went for a swim, cracked his head, then disappeared. Just like the last one. Happens all the time here."

"He can't disappear. They have to find a body."

"He'll be found. We'll make it look like an accident."

"Make it happen," Alderman said. "We'll clean up this mess after. If anyone heard the gunshot shot, it was the generator turning over, got it?"

Both men nodded their heads.

"I'll make sure it's clear." Alderman abruptly left the bungalow.

Monica couldn't believe what she was seeing. She watched as the two men picked up Brenner's lifeless body and carried him toward the door. Alderman returned and said it was all clear, then promptly left and returned in the direction of the theater.

Using the moonlight as navigation, Monica followed behind the men. They carried Brenner's body to a hidden path that vanished into the ferns.

Monica waited a few moments until the men disappeared down the path, and then followed. She was nervous, yet she had to see what they were going to do with him.

Muffled by the white noise coming from the theater, Monica couldn't hear what the men were saying. Suddenly she heard waves crashing on the shore. They were close to the ocean.

The end of the path opened up onto a rocky beach. Monica held back and observed the men carry Brenner onto the rocks. Suddenly Brenner gasped.

He was still alive, barely.

They dropped the body onto the rocks.

"What do we do?" Monica heard a voice say.

One of them pulled out a flask and stuffed it into Brenner's pocket. His body limp, his chest slowly going up and down.

"We have to get him beyond the waves, so the current will drag him out into the open water," Monica barely heard one of the men say to the other. "They'll think he was drunk and hit his head."

The man with the hurt arm picked up a rock and smashed Brenner over the head. He abruptly stopped breathing.

"Just so it looks real, you know?"

"Because he wasn't dead enough already?"

Both men laughed.

A twig snapped beneath Monica's foot. Both men instantly glanced up and saw her. In the glow of the moonlight, Monica locked eyes with theirs. She turned and ran.

30

Jimmy watched Monica touched the dove pendant around her neck as she recounted the events. The charm offered Monica a small amount of comfort, like a crucifix for the religious. Jimmy could tell the event was challenging for Monica to communicate; this was something she had tried to push to the back of her mind.

Jimmy knew a lot about playing tricks with your memory. However, he listened intently to what Monica told him.

"I looked in their eyes right after they bashed Brenner's skull in. I knew they saw me, and it was their eyes that terrified me. They were like white lasers piercing the darkness. The sound was horrible. The crack as the rock smashed into his head." Monica paused. She shivered as if she heard the noise again.

Jimmy wanted to tell her to stop, but he needed to know the entire story. He wanted to see the truth. The two men were clearly Krauthammer and Ramirez, and the sling Jimmy saw Ramirez wearing when he delivered the wine glasses to the island was from the gunshot.

The pieces of the puzzle were starting to come together.

"Brenner might have been saved," Monica continued. "He wasn't dead. I swear, I saw him breathe. He could have been unconscious, just a knock on the head."

"What happened after they saw you?" Jimmy asked.

Monica took one of Jimmy's cigarettes off the table and lit it. "I ran. I could hear them chase me. The ferns slashed me in the face as I tried to find my way up the path. I could hear them saying, 'get her!' and 'we need to get rid of her, fast.'"

Jimmy knew the trauma was still with her by the way she tightened her lips she spoke.

"I knew they would kill me. Smash my head in with a rock or throw me in the ocean as they had done to Brenner and Anna. I had seen the truth. The girls suspected they did the same to Anna, but now it was true. Anna had been murdered. Why? Because they can.

"I eventually made it to the other side of the island, where I hid in some bushes and prayed. I called Eddie and waited. I told him it was dangerous, but he didn't care. He wanted to help me. I knew a place with no cameras." Monica glanced up at Jimmy, tears in her eyes. "That's when he showed up in your boat." She giggled at the thought of that.

Jimmy felt good that she was still able to smile, even if it was at his own expense. A recovery was possible. She was a strong girl, and with enough time could move on with the rest of her life.

"I guess you were too drunk to notice or something." Monica laughed harder. "Eddie said you were buying everyone shots like you were a king or something."

Jimmy nodded and smiled. "Having a good time is one of my weaknesses. I'm glad he put the boat to good use."

"And gave you a ride home." Monica added. "You were passed out in his beach chair at the end of the dock when we got back."

"I'm glad I was the comic relief."

"Thanks, Jimmy."

"It was all Eddie. He's a great guy."

Monica smiled. "I'm lucky to have him."

"You're a special girl, Monica. Soon this will all be over and this will be a distant memory."

"I'm scared."

Jimmy understood. She was safe now, but Alderman was still looking for her. Jimmy knew she needed to get out of St. Thomas. Jimmy couldn't go to the cops; Curtis had done everything he could; buying a ticket and going to the airport was impossible. Jimmy knew Alderman had people paid off at the airport.

What he needed was a private plane to Miami. There was only one person who could help them now.

"You've been through a lot," Jimmy said. "Now it's time to get some rest. Eddie's shift finishes in about an hour and a half. I'm going to pick him up and bring him back here. But there's someone I need to talk to first. I think she might be able to get you off St. Thomas."

The ride to Lisa Brenner's house was easy. The streets were dark and quiet. The little Vespa hurried along through the island hills, the engine working harder with every incline. The breeze felt nice on Jimmy's face, and gave him some time to collect his thoughts. Monica was in danger, but when Lisa knew the truth, that her husband was bludgeoned to death, or so it seemed by Alderman's goons, and that Monica was the only witness, Lisa would help.

Twenty minutes later, Jimmy pulled up to the intercom of the house. Jimmy pushed the button. "It's me. Are you alone? Open up."

Jimmy was hesitant to use his name just in case Alderman was listening. It was his house, after all.

"Okay. I'm alone." Jimmy heard Lisa's voice on the other side. She seemed surprised by Jimmy's arrival.

The large gate opened, and Jimmy sped up the driveway. The door closed behind him. Lisa was already outside when Jimmy got to the house at the end of the driveway. Light from the open front door spilled out into the darkness.

Jimmy tried his best to peer around Lisa to make sure she was, in fact, alone.

"No one's here, James," Lisa said, stepping further into the light, dressed in a simple t-shirt and pajama pants. Lisa's natural beauty was even more evident. "I promise. What is it? You look nervous."

"Your husband was killed."

Lisa gasped. She sat on the front steps, and Jimmy approached her.

"How do you know for sure?" Lisa glanced up.

"I found the girl. She told me what happened."

"Did she have something to do with it?"

"It was Alderman."

Lisa buried her face in her hands, a single tear fell. She pushed her hair behind her head, then looked at Jimmy. "We had our differences, but he was still my husband."

"I know." Jimmy wanted to comfort her, but he didn't feel right doing so. They'd had a strange marriage of convenience that Jimmy didn't understand, but at some time, there had to have been love between the Brenner's.

"Lisa, Alderman is a bad man. He's blackmailing everyone on the island. Using young girls to get them to do what he wants."

Lisa exhaled. "I knew Jonathan was a playboy, but nothing to that degree. But why William? What did he know?"

"Something called the Internet Freedom Act. I don't know everything yet, but it seems like he didn't want your husband to vote a certain way."

Lisa paused. She seemed to know what Jimmy was referencing, even if he had no idea.

"That's what I feared. It wasn't a popular position to take, at least amongst the elites. You should have seen William when he mentioned it at the conference."

Jimmy remembered, but he didn't have the heart to tell her he'd watched it. If this were Lisa's way of mourning, then he would listen.

"They booed him," Lisa laughed. "The son-of-a-bitch walked up on stage and told them all to fuck off. But that was William. He didn't give a fuck about what people thought. For better or worse, it was what I liked about him when I first met him, and then it became for the worst. But that's in the past now."

Jimmy lit a cigarette. Lisa motioned for one, and Jimmy lit hers.

"Where is she?" Lisa asked.

"She's safe. She's been through a lot."

"I bet. I don't want to know about what happened between her and William."

Jimmy understood. William had caused enough pain for her. He wouldn't tell her the exact events if she didn't want to know.

"We need to get her off the island."

"You need a private plane," Lisa said. Her words exactly what Jimmy needed to hear. "Jonathan owns the police, you can't go there either," Lisa continued. "And a commercial flight would be a death sentence for her. We need to be smart, but I can get her off the island. Can she hide out for a few days while I make some calls."

Jimmy nodded. "Lisa, I knew you could help."

Lisa stood up and collapsed into Jimmy's arms. He could feel her heart beating. "Thank you, James. Thank you so much. I both love and hate William. He was good once, I swear."

Jimmy thought about his own past. All those years ago back in Boston, before the tragedy and trial that followed.

"We were all good once," Jimmy said. "I'm trying real hard to be good again."

"We both are."

"This will all be over soon."

"I hope so."

Lisa kissed Jimmy on the lips. "Come inside, stay with me for a little while."

"I don't know."

"Just for a drink. I'm lonely."

Lisa Brenner stood in front of Jimmy. Underneath her pajamas, her body warm and naked. The scent of lavender radiating off her freshly shampooed hair.

Jimmy felt her soft fingers grasp his palm. He could feel her pain, her sorrow, her regret. Two broken people, haunted by their past, and uncertain of the future.

"Just one drink," Jimmy said. The thought of lying down next to Lisa, even for a limited time gave him comfort, like he was not alone in all this. Jimmy followed her inside.

31

Jimmy left Lisa Brenner's house at 10:30 pm. It was a little later than expected, but Jimmy was eager to tell Eddie about their plan when he picked him up after his shift. Lisa had assured Jimmy that she would do everything in her power to keep Monica safe. Alderman may have his connections, but so did William Brenner and, for that matter, Lisa.

Jimmy felt better after seeing Lisa, and for more than the obvious reason. She made him feel calm, at ease with the world. Like it was always just them. They never talked of their pasts. Everything between them existed in the present.

"You can't change the past," she said as they laid next to each other in bed, "and you can't control the future. All who tried drove themselves crazy."

When Jimmy left the house, Lisa kissed him good-bye and said she would have a private plane here in two days. After that, she had a police connection in Miami. Alderman would be brought to justice. Not only for the murder, but the crime of human trafficking.

Jimmy could keep Monica safe for two days. If he had to, he would even bring her to the other side of the island.

Downtown Red Hook was especially boisterous for a Saturday night. Partiers, with cocktails in their hands, spilled out of the Crab Shack onto the street. Red lights and blue lasers shot out from the different clubs.

Jimmy zig-zagged his Vespa through the tourists strolling the street. Beer splashed out of their red Solo cups as they pleasantly stumbled around. Ahead Jimmy saw more lights. This place felt like New Year's Eve. Jimmy believed the red and blue flashing lights up ahead were lasers and disco balls dispersing out from the clubs. But the closer he got, the more he recognized they were police lights. Something was wrong.

There was an accident just before the entrance to the Marooned bar. Jimmy slowed down; he saw an ambulance and police car. A crowd of about fifteen people had gathered at the edge of the road. Some of the onlookers were familiar faces from the bar—a glazed expression in their eyes from the lights' glow and drinking all day.

Kate ran out of the jungle path. She appeared nervous. Her hair bounced with the speed at which she ran. Jimmy followed Kate's eyeline and saw that two paramedics carried what seemed to be a lifeless body from a ditch in the road. Jimmy quickly parked the Vespa on the curb and ran toward Kate.

"What happened?" Jimmy yelled.

"He's dead, Jimmy. Eddie, he's dead." Kate dropped into Jimmy's arms.

Jimmy couldn't believe it. He'd seen Eddie only a few hours ago.

"What happened?" Jimmy asked, clasping Kate by the shoulders.

Tears flowed down her face, the red and blue police lights exacerbating the chaos. "It's all my fault. I did this."

Jimmy didn't know what she was saying. Jimmy immediately ran toward the body. One of the paramedics stopped Jimmy.

"You can't. He's gone," the paramedic shouted.

Jimmy caught a glimpse of the body. It was undoubtedly Eddie. His face bloodied, and his neck turned at an unnatural angle.

"What happened?" Jimmy asked. "How did this happen?"

Suddenly Jimmy felt someone grab his shoulder. The grip was as tight as a vice.

"What are you doing here?" Jimmy heard the deep voice behind him say; he spun him around. Officer Ajax Cason stood in front of him.

"What do you mean, what am I doing here? Eddie was my friend." Jimmy didn't care if Cason was a cop. He was bursting with anger now.

"Well, I'm sorry," Cason said, with bizarre a lack of emotion for someone in his line of work. "I heard he was a good kid."

Officer Cason brushed past Jimmy and threw his massive leather boot over his police motorcycle.

"Jimbo," Cason said. "You're just a tourist down here. Your detective days are over."

Officer Cason waited for the ambulance to pull away, and then he followed them and vanished into the dark winding roads.

There was something off about that man, Jimmy thought. Why did Cason use the word 'detective'? It wasn't a coincidence. Cason somehow knew Jimmy's past, but how much?

Jimmy returned to Kate and put his arm around her.

"I'm to blame," Kate said, burying her face in his chest. "This was my fault."

"Nonsense." Jimmy was beginning to believe there was more to this than what was right in front of him. "What happened? Tell me."

Kate caught her breath and gazed into Jimmy's eyes. "Eddie's shift was over. He said he was going to walk into town to try and find a ride."

Jimmy glanced at his watch. He was late. He knew he could have arrived earlier if he hadn't stayed with Lisa.

"I let him borrow my motorcycle." Kate wiped away her tears and pointed into the ditch at the edge of the road.

At the bottom of the ditch was the remains of a motorcycle. The bike lay in the bottom of the hole like a crumpled aluminum can.

"They said he crashed. That he didn't have his lights on when he pulled out. An SUV hit him."

Jimmy froze. The black Escalade SUV flashed through his mind. Jimmy thought of Krauthammer or Ramirez sitting behind the wheel of that massive SUV and running Eddie down just like he was nothing. Like they almost did with him. Jimmy wondered if they were able to get any information from him.

"Kate, I think Eddie was killed."

Jimmy could feel her body stiffen. "What do you mean?"

"I don't know. I'm trying to figure that out myself."

Out of the darkness, Curtis's pickup truck rounded the bend. Jimmy feared the worst and pulled Kate closer to his body.

Curtis drove the old Toyota pickup truck up next to Jimmy. Curtis looked up from the steering wheel.

"Jimmy," Curtis said. "She's gone."

Kate glanced up from Jimmy's arm. Her face smudged with tears. "Who? Jimmy, what's going on?"

Jimmy didn't know what he feared more, Alderman, or having to tell Kate the truth—the truth doesn't always set you free.

Eddie's death was his fault, not hers. He could have saved him, and now another kid was dead because of him.

Jimmy gazed into the stars above and prayed Monica wasn't dead. He knew he didn't have time to waste. He had to move quickly, decisively.

Death had followed Jimmy Walsh to paradise, but this time he wasn't going to run and hide. He was going to confront it.

If Monica was still alive there was only one place she could be.

Jimmy Walsh looked Curtis and Kate in the eyes and said, "I have to get on that island."

32

"Jimbo, you sure this is a good idea?"

Curtis handed Jimmy a dive mask, and he secured his mask and fins into the boat with the rest of his dive equipment. Jimmy couldn't wait any longer. He and Kate had squeezed into Curtis's small Toyota and raced through downtown Red Hook to get to the Dive Shop and get the boat packed as quickly as possible. Time wasn't on their side. Jimmy knew if Alderman still had Monica on his island, it was only a matter of time before he decided to make her disappear.

Jimmy started the ignition and turned on the lights. "There's no other way. If she's still alive, that's where she'll be.

Kate stepped forward from the shadowed area of the dock. She appeared scared, still in shock of what happened to Eddie.

"What about the police?" Kate asked.

Jimmy shook his head. "Alderman owns the police. Cason was at the crash site. I gotta believe that's how they got to Monica. The island is our only option."

Jimmy glanced at Kate. "I'm sorry I couldn't tell you sooner. I just didn't know. Lisa Brenner has a connection and can get Monica off the island and to Miami in 24 hours. We need to move fast."

Kate folded her arms. "Can you trust Lisa?"

Jimmy wondered that himself, but he had gotten close to Lisa. They had a connection; she was his only option. Jimmy couldn't tell Kate the extent of his relationship with Lisa Brenner. It would just complicate things.

Jimmy nodded his head. "We can trust her." He gazed into the night waters of the Pillsbury Sound. Little Saint George sat quiet and motionless like a distant star.

"Curtis, you getting in?" Jimmy said, nodding to the open seat in the boat. "We have to move fast."

Curtis hesitated; his eyes widened. "I don't know, mon. I got kids, a wife. I can't be playin' James Bond. They got guns, real bullets."

Those weren't the words Jimmy wanted to hear, but he understood. This would be dangerous even if Curtis stayed in the boat; this wasn't Curtis's fight.

"I understand. You've done so much for me already." Jimmy bumped fists with Curtis. He was a great friend and had helped him this far. "Can you make sure Kate gets back?"

Curtis nodded. His face was stern and serious in the moonlight. "Absolutely, mon."

Kate jumped from the dock into the boat. "Not a chance. You can't do this alone, Jimmy. I've known Eddie since he was a kid, and I owe it to him and his family. If you think Alderman did have something to do with his death, then I'm coming."

"Kate, this is dangerous." Jimmy knew she was tough. You had to be to run a bar full of drunk men, but this was different. "These people are serious, killers," he continued. "If they find us, I don't know what they'll do."

"I'm coming. End of story."

By the look in Kate's eyes, Jimmy knew there was no sense in arguing with her. She was stubborn when she had her mind made up.

"Alright. Let's go."

Jimmy put the boat in drive and headed toward Little Saint George.

As they drove toward the island, Jimmy turned off the lights and used the compass to navigate. He filled Kate in with his plan as they made their way across the dark sea. The faint glow of the island lights growing brighter as they approached.

Jimmy anchored the boat on the side of the island where Monica said they didn't have cameras. The spot where Eddie rescued her from the night of Brenner's murder.

"Look in the glove box," Jimmy said to Kate.

Kate opened the latch and glanced inside. A black handgun lay amongst an old nautical map and a few loose cigarettes.

"It's loaded. If anyone comes on board, all you have to do is switch that little button there and pull the trigger." Jimmy pointed to the safety on the side of the gun.

Kate bit her lip. Jimmy knew she was nervous.

Jimmy smiled. "I don't expect anything to happen. I'm going to stay quiet, stay away from people, and just look around. I just want you to know that you can defend yourself if you have to. Understand?"

Kate picked up the pistol and nodded her head. "Yes."

Over the next ten minutes, with the moonlight as his guide, Jimmy put on his wetsuit and got his dive tank and mask strapped to his back. He made sure to carry a backup tank and mask, so if he found Monica, she would have some equipment for the swim back. It was a far swim from the boat to the island. He didn't want to get too close and risk getting spotted.

When Jimmy had all his equipment on, he calmly slipped into the water without a sound.

"Jimmy, you sure you want to do this?"

Jimmy glanced up from the water. He would be lying to himself if he said he wasn't nervous. If Alderman had made Anna Gonzalez disappear and murdered a US Senator, then he wouldn't make an exception for a has-been drunk. Moonlight glistened off the water sparkling across Kate's face; she looked beautiful, strong. Jimmy tried his best to appear confident. There was no sense in making her any more nervous than she already was.

Jimmy thought about his past and how he had failed once. He wasn't going to let that happen again. This time he would rather give his life than live in shame.

"I have to do this," Jimmy mumbled from the water.

Kate nodded. She seemed to understand.

"Be careful, Jimmy."

Kate smiled.

Jimmy put the regulator in his mouth, and cool oxygen flowed into his lungs. Jimmy gave Kate the "OK" symbol and then descended into the black waters.

33

Jimmy shivered in his wetsuit and turned on his flashlight. At night the bottom of the ocean seemed like the surface of an alien planet. Eels and crabs slithered and scurried across the pockmarked ocean floor. The one beam of light emanating from Jimmy's flashlight was his only source of information. No sense of what sea-creature lay behind or to the sides of him, only the five-foot ray of light. The oxygen in his regulator gradually pulsing in and out.

A claustrophobic's nightmare.

Jimmy had been on night dives in the past, but never alone. The first rule a certified diver teaches is never dive alone. It's easy to get into trouble at the bottom of the ocean, and if you're alone, it's inevitable death.

Jimmy's imagination worked overtime. Every scary book or movie Jimmy had ever watched flashed through his eyes: killer sharks, poison eels, swarms of jellyfish. Jimmy glimpsed at the blue glow of his navigation watch. He was on the right path.

Twenty minutes later, Jimmy surfaced at the island's dark, rocky shore. He glanced up. He was at the bottom of a massive cliff. Mixed with the waves crashing ashore, he heard distant muffled sounds of words from above.

Jimmy swiftly dragged his dive equipment to the cliff's base and hid his gear under some dead ferns. Jimmy glanced back out into the water and was relieved he couldn't see his boat. He had successfully made it to shore unseen. Jimmy found a path on the beach's edge that went up to the summit and silently followed it.

His heart beat faster as he crept along the rocky path. Adrenaline like this hadn't pumped through his body in years. However, this time he wasn't afraid or fearful for his life. He had a purpose. As he neared the top, voices grew louder. It seemed like a man was lecturing a woman, but what they said wasn't clear.

Jimmy paused at the top and peered through the ferns that gave him cover. He recognized this area of the compound. Scattered across the perfectly manicured grass were thatched-roofed bungalows. This was the area between the theater and Alderman's compound—the spot where Monica had witnessed Brenner's death.

The orange glow of tiki-torches and pale moonlight lit the area. Jimmy squinted. The man and woman spoke at the entrance of one of the bungalows. No one else appeared to be around.

The man wore a white linen suit and the woman a black evening dress. Both of their faces were shrouded in shadow.

Jimmy moved around the perimeter to see if he could eavesdrop on their conversation.

"You're stunning," Jimmy heard the male voice say.

The voice sounded familiar. As Jimmy grew closer, he saw the face of Jonathan Alderman in the radiance of the flickering tiki-torch.

Alderman brushed the girl's golden-brown hair behind her ear and kissed her. His fingers danced over her petite body. The soft island breeze shifted, and the tiki-torch flame changed direction. A hollow, distant gaze came from the girl. The woman appeared nervous, scared at the presence of Alderman. She was younger than Jimmy had thought. Maybe a teenager.

Alderman grasped the girl's hand then lead her into the bungalow.

Jimmy fought himself from running out into the yard and attacking Alderman right there. Hate bubbled to the surface; Jimmy had lived with years of regret. It ate at him every day.

Alderman must be stopped, but Jimmy knew he had to be smart. No stupid mistakes. He couldn't save Monica and help the other girls if he was dead. Cinderblock tied to his ankles at the bottom of the Pillsbury Sound.

Jimmy took a deep breath and came to his senses. He feared for the girl once she entered the room with Alderman, but he was relieved he could move around the compound more freely.

Except for the breeze and the distant sound of waves crashing ashore, it was quiet. Jimmy made sure to stay in the shadows. Even though the island seemed empty, Jimmy knew Alderman was too smart. He had to have this place wired with cameras.

The principal cameras were easy to spot. Lodged in the top of palm trees, they scanned the compound's interior. Jimmy stayed in the darkness and moved around the cameras as they oscillated back and forth.

He neared the windows of the bungalow Alderman and the girl went into. Jimmy's heart beat faster as he crept closer to the window. Beyond the linen curtains, he saw movement. The shade shifted. Alderman and the girl were on the bed.

Jimmy immediately backed away; he didn't want to see anymore. He moved to the next bungalow, where three nude men lounged in bed chatting and sipping champagne.

Jimmy proceeded further through the ground. His bare feet soft on the recent manicured grass. Sounds of pleasure emanated from the next bungalow. Jimmy peered inside. A man lay naked on the bed underneath a woman. A military uniform thrown on the sea-shell colored sofa caught his eyes. Jimmy had seen that uniform before—the night of the Cyber Talks event. The British officer who had walked by him. That must have been him.

The woman bucked and clawed at the officer, ridding him with everything she had. She howled with delight and gyrated her hips, then thrust her hips forward and threw back her hair, revealing her face through the window for the first time. Jimmy almost collapsed at who he saw.

The woman was Lisa Brenner.

34

Jimmy promptly ducked out of the way for fear of being seen. He dipped below the window and continued to peer through the gap in the linen shade. Lisa gazed out the window with a look of confusion, as if she had seen something.

Jimmy froze.

Lisa's eyes blank and wide, her hair stringy and wet with sweat. Had she seen him? Jimmy didn't know for sure.

A mischievous grin blossomed across her face. Lisa Brenner gazed at herself in the window's reflection, admiring her figure and control of the man underneath. She savored the power she had. Jimmy was relieved she didn't see him; however, dread consumed him. He had seen her gaze of passion before; it had once been meant for him. He felt inadequate, vulnerable. Lisa Brenner had betrayed him.

Suddenly a door opened in the bungalow across the compound.

"Hey!" a voice shouted.

Jimmy halted.

It was Krauthammer.

Massive floodlights on top of the palm trees turned on. Jimmy covered his face with his dive hood as white lights engulfed him and the surrounding area. All that was visible were his eyes; there was no way they could recognize him now. Jimmy sprang to his feet and sprinted to the edge of the clearing.

Jimmy glanced back. Guests began to spill out of their bungalows, adjusting their island-issued bathrobes to appear more presentable to other guests.

Ramirez joined Krauthammer, exiting from the main compound, his arm still in a sling from the gunshot, and ran toward Jimmy. Krauthammer checked his watch. Jimmy assumed he must have a direct video-feed to the cameras all over the island.

Ramirez removed a pistol from the holster concealed beneath his sport coat.

Jimmy retraced his steps down the trail toward the rocky shore. He anxiously hopped over the rocks and roots that blocked his route.

"Stop!" Ramirez shouted. "You got no place to go."

"What's he look like?" Jimmy heard Krauthammer ask Ramirez.

"He wore a mask," Ramirez responded.

Jimmy didn't even stop to put on his dive equipment on once he reached the base of the cliff. He swiftly seized his tanks, mask, and fins, then jetted out toward the dark ocean. He splashed through the soft surf as it rolled to shore, trying to get as deep as possible. Behind him, branches cracked, and Krauthammer cursed as both men tumbled through the undergrowth to get to the bottom of the cliff.

Jimmy had to make it only twenty more feet before dropping into the open ocean. He could sense the water getting deeper as he attempted to wade through the wave.

Bang.

Bang.

Gunfire filled the night. Splashes of water kicked up next to Jimmy.

He looked back. Krauthammer and Ramirez were on the shore. Krauthammer had his pistol raised and his eye on the sight. A flash of white lit the night. The gun fired again. Jimmy sensed pressure on his left arm and then the burning sensation of pain. He was hit. Shock ran through his system. Then the adrenaline took over. He didn't know how bad it was. A throbbing numbing sensation replaced the pain.

Krauthammer fired a second time.

Suddenly Jimmy tasted the water.

His body tensed to prepare for the pain of the second gunshot, but he felt nothing. He had tripped and was now swimming in the water.

Jimmy had made it to the drop off point.

Ramirez fired three more gunshots. All three missing Jimmy and splashing around his head. Jimmy immediately deflated his BCD and strapped his weight belt around his waist.

Suddenly he was darting to the bottom of the ocean like the Titanic. He couldn't breathe. All he saw was the blackness of water. He was safely away from the surface, but none of his equipment was secured as he sank to the bottom. He hoped he hadn't misjudged the depth of the drop-off, and fifteen feet wasn't a hundred feet. Descending that fast was certain death.

Saltwater blinded his eyes. His lungs burned from lack of oxygen. Blindly, Jimmy reached behind him to find the dive tank base. He followed the hose up to the regulator, and he promptly shoved the regulator into his mouth. He cleared the excess water and took a deep breath.

Cold, fresh oxygen roared through his lungs. He could breathe, but he continued dropping into the dark water. Suddenly he slammed into a rock. Jimmy tensed and held onto this tank and regulator. He could live without his fins and mask, but not without oxygen.

Jimmy searched for the valve on his BCD to stop his descent if he fell even further. Jimmy put his hand down and felt sand. He had reached the bottom.

He took a few deep breaths and calmed himself. Panicking now would be the worst thing he could do. Jimmy strapped the BCD on correctly in the darkness of the ocean floor. Jimmy felt for his goggles, which had settled around his neck. He put them on, then cleared the water.

His eyes stung from the salt, but at least he could see. Jimmy glimpsed at his dive watch. The boat was close, but his arm throbbed from the gunshot. He wondered how well he could swim.

Jimmy snapped a glowstick, and the water illuminated with a golden yellow. He sat on the edge of a massive cliff that dropped off into what seemed like infinity. If he had fallen a few degrees off his course, he would be dead. Jimmy dropped the glowstick over the edge and watched it fall. He had expected the glowstick to hit bottom at thirty, then fifty feet, but it never did. It kept falling until it vanished into the darkness.

Jimmy snapped a second glowstick and inspected the gunshot wound. His wetsuit had done an excellent job of keeping the wound together. A streak of blood flowed from the wound like a ribbon of crimson.

He was lucky. The shot had only grazed him. He rolled his shoulder; he could move it.

Something in the distance startled Jimmy. A large grey blur was circling in the open water. His arm wasn't his biggest concern. There was something out there, just off the edge of the drop-off. Jimmy feared what it could be and the scent of blood was in the water.

35

Jimmy removed the dive knife from his belt. Sharks could sense fear. If it did come after him, there was no other option than to fight.

Jimmy glanced at his oxygen gauge. His tank was low, but he still had time before he had to make a move. Jimmy closed his eyes and steadied his breathing. He believed the shark would grow tired of waiting and swim away.

Alone at the Pillsbury Sound's bottom, Jimmy thought of Lisa Brenner. He couldn't get the image of her screaming with pleasure out of his mind. She had to have been behind all of this. Did she want her husband dead? And did she hire Jimmy to track down the only witness, Monica? But why? Jimmy didn't understand.

He glanced at his watch--ten minutes had passed. Jimmy glanced out into the dark open water. He could still see the beast circling round and round, waiting for him to come out. Jimmy could see it was unquestionably a shark now. He couldn't make out what type, but it was big--a man-eater.

Jimmy had to make a move. He couldn't stay down there forever. Either the lack of oxygen or the shark would get him, and he had a chance with the shark. Jimmy pushed off from the ledge into the open water, his knife in one hand and backup dive tank in the other. Jimmy thought the extra dive tank could be used as a shield if it came down to it.

Jimmy knew if he just stayed on this course, he would end up right under the boat. The problem was the shark was directly in his line of sight. Jimmy swam steadily. His arm pulsated in pain, but he pushed through it. There was no other option. Up ahead, the massive beast circled, preparing for its next move. Then as fast as it moved, the shark abruptly disappeared.

Where did it go? Jimmy thought. *There's no way something that big could vanish.*

He frantically looked left and then right.

Nothing.

Jimmy glanced at his navigation watch. He was right underneath the boat. But where was the shark?

Suddenly he felt the full force of the beast crash into him. Its jaws inches from his face as the shark clamped down on his dive tank, barely missing his head. In one quick motion, Jimmy jammed his knife into the snout of the shark. The shark twisted and turned, thrashing in the open water. Jimmy continued stabbing the shark, the water turning red in front of him.

Then just as quick as the shark attacked him, it disappeared. Jimmy's heart raced, fearing another attack, but there was nothing.

Silence.

Jimmy had to move quickly. Get out of the water as fast as possible before it returned for round two, or others showed up. Jimmy glanced at his navigation watch and began his ascent.

"Are you okay?" Kate said as she pulled Jimmy into the boat. "You were down there for a long time. I heard gunshots. I was scared."

Jimmy grunted. If she only knew.

"Oh my god, you're hit," Kate said. "What happened? What did you see?"

Jimmy could barely speak. He clutched his arm; it wasn't as bad as he'd initially thought. Probably just a nasty scar, nothing more.

"It's not that bad."

"Did you find the girl?"

"I didn't have enough time before they caught on to me."

Jimmy still had hope that Monica was somewhere on the island. He imagined her in some cage made out of bamboo with a dirt floor. Jimmy knew he would never get a chance again. The island would be a fortress now.

"Hand me those binoculars?" Jimmy asked Kate.

Jimmy peered through them. Krauthammer and Ramirez were no longer on the shore, but Jimmy could see a flurry of activity on the top of the island. The floodlights were still on, and guards were securing the perimeter.

A light around the dock area of the island turned on. Jimmy knew it wouldn't be long until they had boats out patrolling the shoreline.

"Time to go," Jimmy said and started the boat, then took off towards St. Thomas.

Forty-five minutes later, they were safely back to the Marooned Bar dock.

"You want to stay for a drink?" Kate asked. Her eyes sad, her shoulders slouched. Jimmy could tell she didn't want to be alone, but he couldn't get the image of Lisa out of his mind. He couldn't stay.

Jimmy wrapped his arms around Kate. At first, he appeared to catch her off guard, but then Kate wrapped her arms around Jimmy and cried on his shoulder.

Jimmy wanted to tell her everything, but he couldn't. It felt like there was a knot in his throat.

"I'm sorry," was all Jimmy managed to get out.

Kate pulled back and gazed into his eyes. Her eyes were red from crying.

"For what?" she said.

"Everything."

Jimmy kissed her on the forehead and returned to the boat.

"There's something I have to do."

"Can I come?" Kate asked.

"This is something I need to do alone."

Kate watched from the dock as the dive boat vanished into the Caribbean night.

36

Jimmy sat on the limestone front steps of Lisa Brenner's empty villa. With a cigarette dangling from his mouth, he gazed out at the tropical sunrise. Jimmy rubbed his arm. It was still sore, but more like a bad Charlie-horse than a bullet wound. He had jumped the ten-foot wall encompassing the home to wait for Lisa to return. He was prepared to wait all day if necessary. After last night's events, he guessed Lisa's next move was to leave the island.

The golden sun crested through the overhead ferns, warming Jimmy's bones. His rage at Lisa had receded. He no longer hated her; he pitied her. He was disgusted with her.

The front gate edged open and stirred Jimmy from his daze. A black town car with suicide doors slowly inched through the entrance. The car's tires crunched against the gravel and seashells which made up the driveway.

The car stopped at the end of the limestone walk-way, about twenty feet from where Jimmy sat.

One of the back doors opened, and Lisa Brenner stepped out. Her feet bare, she wore a form-fitting black dress with a shawl covering to keep her warm from the crisp morning air. From her dress to fly-away strands of hair and slightly untidy appearance, Jimmy could tell Lisa hadn't slept all night.

She took a deep breath and approached Jimmy. She halted about five feet away from him. Jimmy waited for her to speak. It was apparent they had figured out he was the one who had been on the island the night before. Jimmy wondered if she knew he had seen her in bed.

"Jimmy," Lisa finally said, rolling the small pebbles beneath her bare feet. It was the first time she hadn't referred to him as James.

Jimmy glanced up from the walkway. They locked eyes for the first time.

"I just came from your place," Lisa said.

Jimmy figured as much. That would have been the first place they would have looked for him.

"I saw you last night." Jimmy exhaled a cloud of smoke. His heart still felt broken, but it was a weight off his chest nonetheless.

"I wish you hadn't seen that."

"Me too."

"You know, everyone has secrets."

Jimmy couldn't deny that, but this felt different.

"Where's Monica?" Jimmy responded.

Lisa glanced back at the black town car. "Come with me."

Jimmy hesitated for a moment but then followed Lisa toward the car. He expected that Monica was in there waiting for him. That all this could finally be over, and he could move on with his life. It was over with Lisa, that was for sure. He couldn't go back to her now. But he imagined Monica's future, leaving the island, moving to the mainland, going to college in Miami or New York—just getting away from all this.

Jimmy climbed into the car and slid across the car's leather seat. Jonathan Alderman and Ramirez sat in the seat directly across from him. There was no sign of Monica.

Alderman had a blank look of defiance on his face; Ramirez, the vacant gaze of a killer. A small silver pistol rested on his knee. The partition between the driver and the backseat was closed behind both men.

"Take a seat," Alderman said.

Ramirez motioned with the pistol.

Lisa shut the door and slid into the car after Jimmy.

"James," Lisa replied as if to reassure him. "Jonathan and I think it would be easier if we all just had a talk."

Jimmy grit his teeth. He had to hold himself back from reaching across the backseat and strangling Alderman to death.

"Where is she?" Jimmy growled.

Lisa gently rubbed Jimmy's arm. "James, please. This has been difficult for all of us."

"Not for all of us." Jimmy glared at Lisa.

Alderman gently tapped the partition. The car began to move down the driveway and out onto the open road.

Lisa glanced at Alderman and then turned toward Jimmy. "Jonathan and I agreed that things would be so much better if everything just went back to the way it was before."

"I can't unsee what I saw last night."

Lisa shielded her eyes; she was embarrassed.

"You can try, can't you?"

"Life doesn't work that way, Lisa. People died. You can't go back." Jimmy couldn't believe how wrong about her he'd been. He could no longer even look her in the eye.

"Of course you can, Mr. Walsh." Alderman adjusted himself in the seat. The silver pistol in Ramirez's hand remained aimed at Jimmy's stomach. "It's only a matter of choice."

"James, please," Lisa begged, "everything would be so much better." She looked at Alderman. Jimmy felt her eyes return to him. "Jonathan spoke with the Governor, and I will replace William as the interim Senator."

Jimmy regretted getting in the car. How could they talk about politics when Monica was still missing? The thought of jumping out of the moving car flashed across Jimmy's mind, but what was the point now?

Jimmy turned to Lisa. "I thought I understood you, but couldn't believe how wrong I was. How can you go along with this? Your husband was killed, two girls are missing, and you're discussing politics?"

"William Brenner's death was an unfortunate accident," Alderman chimed in.

"That's right, James." Lisa sat up straight to show a sign of defiance. She adjusted the shawl over her shoulders. "Jonathan told me everything. I know the truth. I also know William fired his gun first."

Lisa poured a glass of Pinot Grigio from the open bottle on ice. She appeared annoyed now. "William brought that stupid gun everywhere and waved it around like he was James Bond. Every time he had a few drinks in him, he thought he was untouchable. I was always afraid of something stupid happening.

"Please, James," Lisa begged again. She leaned in close. Jimmy could feel her breath against his ear. "Jonathan left a significant amount of money in the glove box of your boat. You'll be able to start all over again. Buy your own business."

Jimmy thought of Monica.

"So I'll be bought off, and you'll be another puppet Senator?"

"Don't be naive, Mr. Walsh." Alderman poured Jimmy a glass of wine.

Jimmy refused.

Alderman shrugged, then raised his glass to Lisa and said, "The world needs people like Mrs. Brenner and me."

"Second chances don't come around often," Lisa said. "We have to look out for ourselves."

"You think money is going to stop me from talking? What about Monica? Where is she?"

"No, Mr. Walsh," Alderman responded. "That was a sign of good faith. This will stop you from talking."

Ramirez handed Alderman a laptop, which he subsequently turned towards Jimmy.

Alderman twirled the stem of the empty wine glass between his left hand, took a sip and said, "You've been running all over the island with that pendant playing detective. How long do you think until people start asking questions: why did he go to that Dove school?" Alderman grinned as he chose his words carefully. "What does he traffic on that boat of his? All I have to do is release this footage and then it all comes back to you. Who's going to believe a disgraced cop?"

Alderman refilled his glass, grinned and said, "Checkmate."

37

Jimmy watched the videos on the laptop. Security footage of himself snooping around the Freedom Dove House. He saw Joni's video at the Dive Shop from the night Jimmy drove Monica to the island, followed by footage of Monica with Senator Brenner.

"Turn it off," Jimmy said and looked away.

"You see, Mr. Walsh, I have a backup plan. Trafficking underage girls for a United States Senator is a terrible crime. Especially when his death is still an open investigation."

"That will never fly in court."

"Oh yes, it will, especially with my connections and Lisa's support. Who wouldn't pity the wife of a terrible man, especially a US Senator drunk on power?" Alderman closed the laptop and continued, "Are they doing to listen to you? An alcoholic loser cop responsible for the deaths of multiple children? No. What jury would believe you? Jimmy, go home, buy a new boat, and start debt-free. Forget this even happened."

The rage burned in Jimmy. He had to do something. Suddenly, he lunged at Alderman. Ramirez's massive frame quickly caught Jimmy and pushed him to the ground. Jimmy attempted to fight Ramirez off, but there was no chance. Ramirez pinned him down and, like a vice-grip, squeezed his arm. Blood poured out, staining his shirt.

"You won't be as lucky next time," Ramirez whispered into Jimmy's ear.

"This is how you type of people get away with it, right?" Jimmy winced under Ramirez's weight.

"You take one of my two offers," Alderman said. His voice calm and methodical. "I would prefer the first. We both leave happy and, for your sake, alive. Please decide promptly. Me and Mrs. Brenner have a plane to catch. After all we have to start laying the groundwork for a political campaign." Alderman chuckled. "Who knows? Maybe in a few years, she'll be running for President."

The car jolted to a halt. Alderman opened the door, and a burst of Caribbean heat entered the air-conditioned vehicle.

"Unfortunately, Mr. Walsh, this is where our story ends. It was nice meeting you, and I look forward to never seeing you again. I take it enough blood has been spilled? Go, enjoy the money. Live the rest of your shitty little life in peace."

"Where's the girl?" Jimmy scowled at Alderman.

Alderman smirked. "Word of advice, Mr. Walsh— let it go." Alderman tapped Jimmy on the shoulder and said, "Don't be so hard on yourself. After all, this is paradise."

Jimmy looked at Lisa. "You know. Where is she?"

Lisa shielded her eyes as if she couldn't bear to face the truth and said, "Goodbye, James."

Suddenly Jimmy felt the air rush as Ramirez threw him out of the car. Jimmy slammed against the pavement, but he managed to put his hands down before smashing his face into the asphalt. From the ground, Jimmy looked at Lisa. There were tears in her eyes. He didn't know if they were meant for him, Monica, or the guilt she felt.

"Please," Jimmy pleaded. He wanted her to help him to do the right thing.

Lisa turned away and shut the door.

The driver's side window went down. Jimmy slowly got to his feet and walked toward the window. Krauthammer handed Jimmy a piece of paper, then abruptly put up his window and drove away.

As the car pulled away, Officer Ajax Cason drove his motorcycle out of a nearby area about one hundred feet ahead, hidden by ferns. Cason abruptly put on his police siren, acting as an escort as the town car sped down the long winding island road.

Jimmy glanced at the piece of paper. A set of longitude and latitude coordinates were scribbled on it. Jimmy slowly lifted his head and gazed out into the endless Caribbean Sea.

Grief overtook Jimmy at the significance of the co-ordinates. He knew they were the final resting place of Monica Diaz.

Suddenly, a strong breeze snatched the small piece of paper out from Jimmy's hand and carried it toward the ocean.

Jimmy imagined Monica resting silently at the bottom of the ocean, her body swaying back and forth in the gentle current of the Pillsbury Sound. The dove pendant necklace safely fastened around her neck while creatures nibbled at her flesh and crabs crawled, pecked at her toes.

Jimmy fell to his knees and retreated to the darkest part of his mind.

38

A few days later, Jimmy Walsh pulled his Vespa up to the Marooned Bar. Clean-shaven and wearing a collared shirt, he had had time to digest the events of the past two weeks.

A sign reading "CLOSED" was hung in front of the path that led to the bar. Jimmy heard the sound of a TV in the distance. He pushed the sign aside and went through.

Kate stood at the empty bar, slouched watching the TV.

"You want something to drink?" Kate nodded, almost expecting him.

Jimmy shook his head. "No thanks. Drying out a bit."

Jimmy glanced up at the TV in the corner of the bar. The news played—helicopter footage of a large political rally.

"You hear the news?" Kate said.

Jimmy watched as the news footage changed to a closeup of Lisa Brenner. Dressed in conservative attire Lisa addressed the crowd of people. To her left stood Congresswoman Reilly, and in the background, Jimmy could make out Jonathan Alderman amongst the other suits.

"It is with humility that I accept the appointment of US Senator to this great state." Lisa bellowed in front of the crowd. "I will do my best to live up to my husband's legacy, and that is why I will support the *Internet Freedom Act!*"

The crowd erupted in applause.

"Protecting our children is investing in our future. We cannot allow hate and xenophobia to pollute the internet and destroy our future."

Jimmy reached for the remote an arms-lengths away and shut the TV off.

"I'm not one for the news."

"I don't blame you."

Jimmy adjusted the small bag of cash that Alderman had given him." I've been thinking about a change of scenery."

Jimmy and Kate sat in the silence of the empty bar, looking into each other's eyes. He could sense her pain, but there was a glimmer of hope.

Kate scanned the empty bar, then returned to Jimmy. She crossed her arms. "You come here to ask me something?"

"I'm not a good man, but I'm not a bad one either."

Kate reached out and touched Jimmy's hand. "We all have a past. Paradise is not what it seems, huh?"

Jimmy gazed into Kate's eyes and smiled.

"It all depends on who you spend it with."

J.D. Krueger

THE END